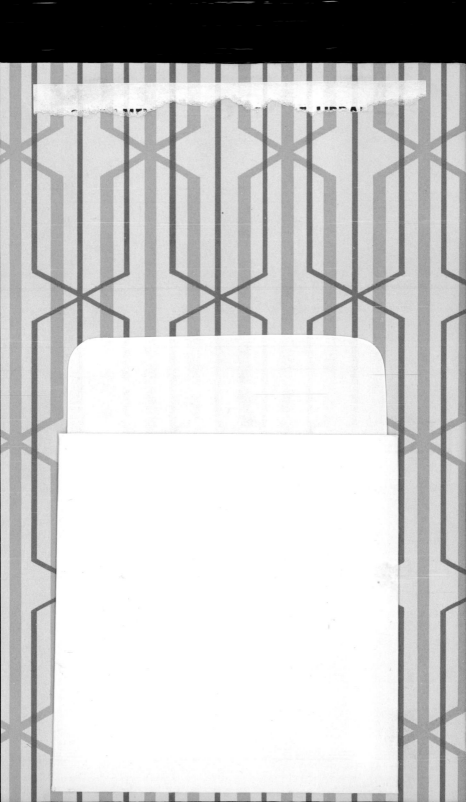

TALES OF
DUNSTABLE WEIR

TALES OF
DUNSTABLE WEIR

By
GWENDOLINE KEATS
(ZACK, PSEUD.)

Short Story Index Reprint Series

BOOKS FOR LIBRARIES PRESS
FREEPORT, NEW YORK

First Published 1901
Reprinted 1969

STANDARD BOOK NUMBER:

8369-3116-5

LIBRARY OF CONGRESS CATALOG CARD NUMBER:

70-94736

CONTENTS

TALES OF
DUNSTABLE WEIR

BENJAMIN PARROT'S FANCY

I NEVER heard tell that furreners thought much of Dunstable Weir, as a place to live in, till old Benjamin Parrot came back along home from Australia and promised to leave all his money—he was most amazing rich—to the first man that took his fancy; but no sooner did the news get abroad than the price o' houses went up, there wasn't building room to contain the folk, and the village bid fair to become a town. It seemed a bit hard to me and t'others who had been born and bred in the parish, and us didn't give these extry lumps no special welcome; for, though they started a "tea-totalers'" club and Band o' Hope teas, us had always been well content wi' the ale

at the Red Lion afore, and us didn't no-
ways feel less willun' to bide by it arter us
had smacked our lips over their new-fangled
brews.   Benjamin Parrot watched 'em all
out o' his small ferret eyes wonderful unconsarned, and it soon became pretty clear
that the man that shud take his fancy hadn't
put his foot inside the village.   Law bless
'ee, they didn't lose heart, not they—they
busticumed the more, that's what they did.
The charch o' Dunstable Weir wor mortal
old and fally-to-piecey, they patched un up
on the outside—well, us didn't complain o'
that, 'tiddn't noways comfortable to be
fetched out o' a quiet snooze by a big drap
o' rain pat 'pon tap the crown o' your head ;
but not content they tarns a good job into a
bad un, and cuts down all the pews inside o'
the charch so that everyone could see everyone else—a kind o' prying that no self-
respecting body in Dunstable Weir would
have demeaned to afore.   Well, then they
buckles to and puts a banging great stove in

the middle o' the aisle, over agin Benjamin
Parrot's pew.   Warmth in reason is a thing
I'm the last to complain of; but the charch
was terrible small and the stove terrible big,
and the first Sunday it was lit Benjamin
Parrot was forced to off wi' his coat and sit
in his shirt-sleeves.   'Twasn't long arter that
the flooring gived way, and stove and all
fell quat on top o' the Squire's old Aunt
Jane, who had been lying a peaceful corpse
there twenty years.   It was this same winter
—and a bitter cold winter it was that
Martin Fippard's wife fell sick and died.
No one knowed 'zactly what 'twas that
carried her off, more'n that it was a persistent sickness with a deal o' cling about it.   I
was present at her taking, and though I be
partial to death-beds, folks being wonderful
much theirselves at such times, there seemed
a bit too much human nature about Susan
Fippard's.   Her wasn't noways old when
her died, close upon her thirty-ninth year or
thereabouts, and being well-featured was

personable to the last. It was always a matter of curiosity in the village what 'twas that made her take to Martin, a terrible plain man wi'out a plain man's tongue; but there's no denying her was mortal fond o' un, as he was willun' to be o' her, only, owing to the contrariness o' things, he couldn't get beyond simillication. Folks said—but they tell up such lies—that he had acted unfaithful from the first. Be that as it may there was one little twig o' a woman, Belle Hart was her name, and Susan Fippard couldn't abide the sight o' her. The queer thing was that though no mortal soul ever saw Martin go nigh the maid, the village all agreed 'long o' Susan that there be times when folks' eyes be to let, and there be more to be zeen than be zeed. It zim'd to me that if once they'd been caught together, folks wouldn't o' been so terrible sure they was guilty, but it was just the never finding 'em out that made things look so special black. Not that folks was wishful

to spare pains over the matter, and they laid
most as many traps for Martin as they did
for the fancy o' Benjamin Parrot. I reckon
myself that the village was mistook, and
didn't zee nought, because there was nought
to zee ; but I niver said so, not holding con-
tradictiousness recommendatory in a single
man such as I be. Martin took things
wonderful quiet; there was times when I
couldn't help but wonder if he knowed that
all the village was on the watch for un.
But he was never speechful, and grew more
word-shy with years. There was only one
street to Dunstable Weir ; it straggled over
the best part o' two hills, the river running
atween 'em. Over agin the bridge the
houses fell sort o' back from the road, one
banging great allum * standing up by hisself
on a patch o' green over against the Red
Lion Inn. A few paces away, on t'other side
o' the road, was Belle Hart's cottage. Five
stone steps led to the door; they was a bit

* Elm.

worn in places, but the hand-rail was sound
and painted pea green, and the rest o' the
wood-work was coloured the same. Belle
was a milliner by trade, though her used her
needle for other odd jobs, such as the making o' new coverings for the Squire's seat in
charch, and bags for the Hall hams. Her
could be seen most days sitting aside her
window sewing, plainer in winter than t'other
times because by then the fuchsias had died
back a bit. Most o' us would drop in now
and awhile at the Red Lion for a glass o'
beer, but Martin never came 'cept Saturday
nights, then just as the charch clock struck
the quarter after eight us would hear un
coming over the cobble-stones—one o' his
legs was a bit shorter than t'other and gave
a draggy sound to his walk, so us always
knowed 'twas he. When he got opposite
Belle Hart's cottage he'd stop a bit and look
in ; most like the blind ud be down, and
there ud be the shadder o' the little woman
thrawed acrass. Us over at the Red Lion

used to unbutton our eyes, but us never saw
nought worth seeing; the little shadder that
maybe had been bobbing and twisting a
moment afore would bide stone quiet, then
Martin ud move on and the shadder wud
brisk up and flit about as shadders will.
Martin wasn't noways a sociable man; he'd
throw down his bit, take his glass, go out
and nivver say a word, not as much as "good
evening" to any o' us. The village didn't
think well o' such silence, holding that 'twas
a queer thing a man so much telled about
should have nought to tell back. Some
reckoned 'twas shame kept un to silence, but
I think myself 'twas just the nature that was
in him. Not that there wasn't contradic-
tious points to Martin; he was a careful
man, never laying out a penny where he
wasn't fo'ced, but he didn't take no special
interest in Benjamin Parrot, leastways not
first-along; and when I said 'twas a scan-
dalacious thing o' they furren lumps to come
here sniffing round after gold, just as if Dun-

stable Weir was public property the same
as South Africa, he only answered that
"Mostlike they wud bring more money
into the village than they'd ever succeed in
taking out o' it." Zim'd a poor-spirited
fashion o' looking at matters, but he wasn't
no patriot, taking no interest in war or the
grasping ways o' t'other nations, though
there was not a child in the parish who
couldn't have told him that if 'twasn't for
England there would be little enough hon-
esty left in the world, or religion either for
the matter o' that. At election times he
never went near the Red Lion, but just bided
at home; and when the Squire had us all up
to the Great House to dinner and said he
hoped that we'd all "vote straight," Martin
got up and said, "What was straight for one
wasn't always straight for t'other," which
the village held, for a silent man, was saying
a deal too much. Farmer Burden was terrible put out, Martin being carter to he, and
went so far as to ax if the Squire was wish-

ful to have Martin turned away; but the
Squire wouldn't hear o' it, and because o'
that there be some who reckon the Squire's
own politics iddn't sound.

Well, curious to relate, the one man that
Benjamin Parrot took note of was none
other than Martin, though to be sure, what
wi' this thing and that, the village fair
twanged wi' his name. Folks would have
twittered louder had they known whose
fancy he was like to take, but each o' 'em
was so sure that he himself was the man,
that 'twas some time afore they suspicioned
the truth. Benjamin Parrot lived in a big
house at the far end of the village; he was
a big man hisself by nature, wi' the dropsy
which made un bigger. His legs swelled so
toward the last that he was forced to get
the carpenter to make un a wheel chair, and
he paid me sixpence an hour to draw it. Us
always went the same way, down one hill,
'cross the bridge and up t'other side. When
us passed Belle Hart's cottage Benjamin

Parrot would fit the tips o' his fingers together and say,—

"So this is where the woman lives that all this to-do's about, eh?"

Arter a bit us would come round by Martin's, and old Parrot 'ud stop again.

"And here's t'other woman's cottage," he'd continny. "Do 'ee reckon there's any truth in the tale, Zack?"

"Well," I answered, scratching my head to ease out the words, "me and the village be one and the same mind in public, but when I gits by myself I has a single man's judgment."

It was jest about this time that Susan Fippard fell sick, though maybe her had been ailing longer than us thought. Her began life mortal proud, and such iddn't the first to show when the world goes ill wi' 'em; but there was sommat in her stronger than pride, and thic was jealousy. A banging, great-hungered, wide-bellied thing; you could see most her pride fall away bit by bit afore it, till her didn't seem to have no self-respect left. Drink and jealousy be much o' a muchness, and one 'ull bring folks as low as t'other. The village was terrible took up wi' watching, though they all said 'twas a poor sight to see. I was sorry for the woman, having gone droo sommat the like myself at one time, but 'tiddn't no great tale and I reckon 'twill die wi' me. Folks say, though I can't swear to the truth o' it, that her went down on her knees and begged Belle Hart not to take Martin away from her, and Belle just stitched and stitched and answered nary a word. After all the maid hadn't done nought, but folks didn't blame her the less for that.

When it became as plain as spring in May that Susan was marked for death, no one pitied her much, holding that she had brought it all on herself, and if Martin had spoke up bold and throwed all the blame on his wife there was more'n one person in Dunstable Weir who would have stood his friend. But he didn't say nought, and the village held the silence for unhandsome and never forgived un for it. About this time he gave up coming to the Red Lion o' Saturdays, and when his work brought un that side o' the bridge he never so much as dropped a glance on the little green-painted windy where Belle Hart sat all alone to herself sewing. Well, as I said before, 'twas terrible cold that winter, the snow came chunking down and nipped off the tree-tops, just for all the world as if they was so many heads o' cabbage. Martin's cottage stood higher than the rest o' the houses and more open to the weather, the thatch was bulged down wi' the weight on top o't and the snow drifted up in the corner o' Susan's bedroom so Martin was fo'ced to take her down to the kitchen to die comfortable and warm. I was out of work about then, it bein' a deal too cold for Benjamin Parrot to take his ride in the chair, so I made a point o' dropping in to ax how Susan did, part from curiosity and part because it was cheaper to sit aside a neighbour's fire than light one o' my own. The weather made folks fair scared o' going outside their doors, and I never was in a house at such a time when there was less company on the watch, so to speak. Her died on a Friday, getting on for six o'clock. It had been dimmet* since a quarter afore three, the sky was that packed wi' snow. Farmer Burden he gave Martin a holiday, there bein' next to no work doing, so he and me us sat one on each side o' the fire, and Susan her lay stretched out on the bed, wi' her face turn'd to the wall most o' the time. Us was silent, not having nought particular to say. After a bit I fell into a doze, and when next I opened my eyes Martin had turned round in his chair and was facing Susan. Her was sitting up straight, looking terrible full o' life, though there wasn't much more than an hour of it left in her. One big loop o' hair had

* Twilight.

got loose from the rest, and her wound it around her fingers and twisted it up quick and irritable, though I reckon myself her didn't know what her was doing.

"Pramise," her said, "pramise."

But he sort o' held back.

"Pramise her sha'n't come here after I be gone."

Martin moved uneasy-like, crossing and uncrossing his legs. He was a big man, wi' a big face wonderful scanty o' looks.

"Her's never worked 'ee no harm," he said at last.

"Pramise, and then I shall die quiet."

He didn't make no answer, but I heard the fingers o' his great hands crack as he twitched 'em apart.

"'Tis cold out there, Martin," her said, "mortal cold and dark."

"Ay," he answered, "it's been freezing these dree weeks and more."

I could see the beads o' sweat standing out on the face o' un for all that.

"Martin," her cried, shrill - like, "you pramised to be faithful to me afore the altar."

"And I have been true to 'ee, Susan."

"But you and her will ha' killed me between 'ee."

He sat stone quiet, and if he looked about for words, he didn't find 'em.

All to-wance her held out her arms to un. "You iddn't glad o' it? You iddn't glad I be leaving 'ee—"

He rose up and went to her and put his arms round her poor thin body terrible pitiful, but he didn't answer, and kaining across at 'em I saw sommat o' what it is to be wi'out the gift o' words. I reckon, though, her understood un better'n I did, for her seemed sort o' comforted.

"You've been a good husband to me, Martin, in spite o' it all," she said.

He gave a banging great sob, and the sound o' it seemed to take the life out o' her. "I'll no axe it o' 'ee. Marry her if you

will "—and wi' that her face stiffened, and
she fell back dead.

Martin he stood a-looking down on her,
then he took her hand in his and called me
up to the bedside.

"Zack," said he, "you be my witness that
I promise never to marry t'other woman."

"I wudn't pass my word on it if I was
you," I answered, being no friend to rash
promises.   But he didn't pay no heed.

"See," he said, taking me by the arm,
"her's heard."

Sure enough, her did look more content-
like.

I hiked off down to the Red Lion, for I
felt that a drop o' sommat warm and speech
wi' ordinary folk would be a relief.   The
bar was well-nigh full o' men stamping the
snow off their feet so as to give the liquor
they'd swallowed time to trickle into the
right place afore they went back once more
to work.   When I had told my tale two or
three times over from start to finish, someone

proposed us should step across to Belle
Hart's cottage and hear what her had to say
to it.

Us trapesed in wi'out stopping to knock.
She was sitting afore the fire sewing. Her
throwed a terrible scornful look out o' her
black eyes—I reckon myself her knowed
what had brought us.

"Well," her said, "be the church on fire,
and have 'ee come for blankets to put it
out?"

"No," us answered, "Martin's wife be
dead."

"And what's that to me," she said, "that
you should take upon yourselves to burst
open my door wi'out so much as a 'By your
leave'?"

I felt a bit sorry us had come, for there
was no mistaking that us looked amazing
foolish, standing gapnesting across at her.
Then one o' 'em pushed me forward.

"Zack 'ull tell 'ee all about it," he said.

I wasn't altogether pleased wi' the job set

for me. "Her died comfortable at the last,"
I said, edging away a bit. Belle turned
away that small head o' hers so us couldn't
see nought but the braids o' her black hair,
that was coiled up neat and glossy.

"Poor soul," her said softly, "poor soul."

"Zack hasn't telled 'ee all," the great gaw-
ken bawled out, the same man that had
spoke afore.

"Do the telling yourselves," I answered,
for I was fair sick o' the business.

So they telled her.

"Be that all?" her axed, quiet-like.

"Ess," they answered.

"Then maybe you'll go out the way you
came in," her said.

And us did, feeling amazing subdued over
so small a matter.

Well, wi' the burying o' Susan the
weather fell round once more to soft, and I
went back to work at Parrot's. The old
man was a deal more interested to hear o'
Martin's promise than iver Belle Hart had

been, and made me tell un the tale over and over again.

"Do 'ee reckon he'll bide by his word, Zack?"

"I can't say," I'd answer.

Benjamin Parrot 'ud fit the tips o' his fingers together.

"I like a man that sticks to his promise, but—" and he'd stop short and end to hisself, "Fippard should ha' thought o' t'other woman."

Spring dropped round, and what wi' the shooting o' the crops, and birds calling one to t'other, there was a wonderful lot o' nature about. Martin's blood seemed to quicken under it, for he started to visit Belle Hart open, and 'twasn't long before it got whispered abroad that he was about to put out o' mind all that he had said so mortal solemn on the day his wife died. The whole village cried shame on un, though, as far as that goes, no one could say if there was truth in the tale or not.

Over against Martin's cottage there was a tiddleliwinkie* bit o' a wood, the road ran along the lower end o' it, wi' a narrer path that led up through the trees. 'Twas close to this spot, one arternoon late in spring, that I came on Martin and Belle sort o' unawares. I was out wi' the chair, and the old man, his head lolling on tap his shoulders, had dropped off into a doze. Being mortal weary o' always ding-donging along the same bit o' road, I waited till I saw he had bitten well into his sleep, and then I wheeled un up the side track through the trees. Well, us hadn't gone far afore I catched sight o' Martin's broad shoulders. I knew well enough who 'twas, because o' late he had taken to wearing a brown coat week-a-days that he had hisself patched wi' green. Unconscious-like I went a bit softer, and the next moment who should step out from among the trees but Belle. Then I stopped quat and the old man woke up

* Insignificant.

and glowered about un, but zeeing, no doubt, who there was in front he bided as silent as a stone. Martin and the maid was that took up one wi' t'other they didn't pay no heed to aught else. Her sat down 'pon tap a big log and Martin stood 'long side o' her. Not a word passed the lips o' either o' 'em, and I was jest thinking to myself that for sweethearts they made a terrible poor display, when all to-wance Martin fell to cursing. He cursed hiszulf and folks in general, and the maid; he cursed the tongue atween his teeth, which zimed proper enough considering the use he was putting it to—he cursed God Almighty—a thing I had never known no man in Dunstable Weir ha' the face to do afore. Belle Hart her sat there and listened, not a finger did her hold up to keep the words back from coming, though I cud zee her small white face grow sort o' smaller and whiter afore my eyes. All of a minute the wuds stopped o' theirzulves, and he flung his arm round the branch o' a tree and

leaned his vace up agin it. Then 'twas that
Belle riz and went over to 'un, but he flung
her off becase, he said, that if the dead cud
hear maybe they cud zee as well, and wi'
that he fell to laughing in a fashion that
was amazing disquietful for them that cudn't
enter into the joke. The maid kained across
at un rather pitying, and I reckoned arter a
bit maybe her'd say sommat to make un give
over sich show-sides, but her jest tarned and
hiked off through the wood. I drawed the
chair back tenderful the way us had come,
for 'twasn't no manner o' use gapnesting at
Martin. The day arter that the old man
didn't feel over-well, and had me up to his
room. 'Twas the smallest in the house, and
poked away over the back kitchen. Nought
hung on the wall 'cept an old calendar and a
soft black hat wi' a clay pipe stuck in the
band; but a bed stood in one corner, a
chest o' drawers in t'other, while atween
'em and the door was a table and a candle-
stick bang in the middle of it. The vanty-

sheeny * furniture was all away in the front part o' the house, which, arter all, was where it shud ha' been, and Benjamin Parrot lying there in the bare tiddleliwinkie room didn't zeem so terrible much out o' place either.

"Zack," he says, as I pulled a lock o' hair to un, because, when all was done, I was in his employ, "what sort o' a man be this Martin Fippard? Do he think much o' money?"

"More'n most," I answered, "though for the matter o' that all o' us likes the feel o' siller atween our wants and ourzulves."

"Well," said Benjamin Parrot, "if he acts the way I wish, he can be donc wi' sich things as wants, for I'll make the man my heir."

"Begore," I tummil'd out, "if things are to be settled thic easy, there's more'n one o' us that would give 'ee satisfaction."

A curious smile crossed the old man's face, but he made as if he hadn't heard.

* Showy.

"Let un marry Belle Hart and the money's his."

"Why, dom it," said I, "iddn't that what he's been arter doing all along?"

"There's his promise to his dead wife."

"When I drop un a word o' what you say I reckon 'twill be your promise, not hers, he'll be thinking upon."

Benjamin Parrot zot up in the bed. "You'll keep what I tell 'ee to yourzulf," he tapped out sharp.

"'Tiddn't possible; a janius couldn't be answerable for sich, much less ordinary folk zame ez I be."

The old man let fly another o' they curious smiles o' his.

"Oh, yes, Zack," he said, "you'll bide silent because"—and he stopped quat and fitted the tips o' his fingers terrible careful each to each—"because if Martin don't git the money maybe you will."

"Lord help us," I answered, sinking down 'pon tap the bed, "there shall be no silenter man inside the village or out o' it than my-zulf."

"Ah," piped old Parrot, "I knowed I cud trust 'ee under the circumstances."

From that time on I felt sort o' different toward Martin Fippard. I'd never seen aught to mislike in the man afore, but now 'twas much as if he was a-trying to keep me out o' my own. I watched un suspicious, and 'tis wonderful how black folks' ways 'ull look the moment you give over trusting 'em.

To show me clear enough that the Almighty was much o' the same mind, it was at this identical moment that Martin's old black sow took upon herzulf to die in straw, and her whole litter had to be raised by hand, which made away with a lot o' the profit. Martin was terrible put out over it; it was a deal o' money, and he was a careful man. He axed me to sit up wi' her one night so that he might snatch a bit o' sleep hisself; but the poor critter was that bad wi' the spazams that 'twas more'n one man's

work to hold her, so he was forced to bide
up jest the same. 'Twas a wet night, and
the roof of the sty leaked painful; me and
Martin was humped up in one corner wi' the
sick sow atween us, and an old horn lantern
hanging from a nail above our heads. The
light fell on Martin's face, and I could see
he was thinking hard, as well he might at
such a time.

"Zack," he said all to-wance, "do 'ee
reckon that Benjamin Parrot be so terrible
rich as folks give out?" I was rather taken
aback, because I reckoned that he was going
to say sommat about the sow, or Belle Hart,
or maybe both of 'em together.

"Whativer makes 'ee ax such a question?"
I said.

Martin ran a finger and thumb through
his bristly red beard.

"Because he tells me that I be the sort o'
man he could fancy."

"Lord ha' mercy on us, why should un
take a fancy to the likes o' you?" I spoke

more than usual sharp, because it kind o'
gave me a stab to hear the name o' Parrot
in Martin's mouth 'tall.

"That I can't tell 'ee," Martin answered;
"I only know what he said."

"And what did he say?" I axed.

"He said that if I tarned out to be the man
he took me for, he'd leave me all his money."

"A likely game thic," I said; "what do
he take 'ee for?"

"If you could tell me thic, I should know
what to be after," said Martin.

After that us was silent a bit, for the old
sow fell into one o' her spazams, and us and
her was all over the sty. When the fit was
past, and Martin had pulled some o' the
straw out o' his hair and eyes he turned to
me.

"Zack," he said, "do 'ee reckon Benjamin
Parrot has heard tell o' that promise I made
Susan?"

"'Twould be a queer thing if he hadn't,"
I answered.

"Well, has that aught to do wi' it?"

"Why should it ha' aught to do wi' the matter?" I tummil'd out hasty, for hadn't I promised to keep the old man's secret?

But Martin was fixed to the subject. "If so be I was to marry again," he said.

My heart banged up agin my ribs, and then stopped quat—

"He wouldn't leave 'ee the money, I s'pose," I answered. The wuds slipped out unconscious, for I hadn't a mind to say aught sich.

Martin breathed a bit hard. "That's how I reckoned it out myself," he said. "Good Lord!" he added sharp-like, looking down at the old sow that was lying wi' her legs crossed like the crusader in Dunstable Weir charch; "her's 'parted!"

Sure enough, her was dead.

"'Tis a terrible pity that the selling o' sich as bacon is agin the law," Martin muttered to himself, taking the lantern down from the peg and blowing out the candle.

"Well, there iddn't nothing to be said against your eating her," I answered short, for it seemed to me he might have left the light burning a bit longer, leastways till us was out o' the sty, which wasn't over clean.

"I shall that," he said, "but I'd a deal rather ha' the money safe in my pocket."

Martin didn't go nigh Belle Hart's cottage for three or four weeks arter that, and when Saturday came round he niver so much as put a foot inside the door o' the Red Lion. I met un whiles and again, and I thought to myself that he missed the spirits, though 'twas nought but a glass once in seven days, for his face had a divorced anxious look on it. I reckoned 'twud be safer to let the village know that Benjamin Parrot had spoke o' making Martin his heir, though I didn't tell 'em the conditions, having, so to speak, promised faithful to keep 'em to mezulf. Folks was none too pleased, for they couldn't a-bear the thought o' un coming in for Benjamin Parrot's money, and at the same time

they was curious to see what ill would befall
Martin if he broke his promise to Susan. It
was just about now that Farmer Burden's
daughter came home. Her'd been up to
Exeter to learn the millinery trade, and
brought a 'mazing lot o' bonnets and female
trash back 'long wi' her. The women was
pleased to have their hats and sich trimmed
by someone t'other from Belle, because they
said there was too much talk about Belle
for her to be as respectable as her should be.
So, after that, few folks knocked at the little pea-green door, and Belle sat aside her
windy wi' her hands in her lap most days.
Her seemed to be thinking a deal, which
iddn't good for maids, they, poor souls, not
being built for sich. I dropped in once and
axed her to make me a new tie for Sundays
out o' a bit o' red and yeller striped satin
that I'd bought cheap into Barnstaple Fair,
for I couldn't abide to see they small fingers
o' hers so mortal still. While I sat and
watched her working, who should come to

the windy and gape in, but Martin. Her didn't look up, but I reckon her knowed right enough who was there, for her stitched terrible fast. After a while he hiked off. I never was able to wear that tie, for 'twas made so inventive I cudn't git into it. When I drawed old Benjamin Parrot past the little pea-green windy thic zame arter-noon he tarned to me and said,—

"So Martin hasn't married her yet?"

I didn't make no answer, becase luck is a contrary thing, and the moment you reckon 'tis on your side it skips acrass to t'others.

One dinner hour, as I was sitting down to a slice o' bread and bacon, and thinking to myself that 'twasn't often a single man had a hot meal, when, who should drop in but Martin. 'Twas a goodish while since I'd set eyes on un, and I marked that he hadn't grown younger wi' time.

"Zack," he tumbled out, sort o' breathless, "they tell me her's to be sold up."

I knew well enough that he was speaking

o' Belle Hart, because I'd heard the same tale from more pair o' lips than one; but feeling a bit unfriendzome toward Martin I took another munch at the bread and bacon afore answering.

"Well," I said at last, "I don't see that it much matters to you if her be, considering that you iddn't going to get married to her."

"Then, it's true," he exclaimed, and wi' that he sat down quat on the only bit o' butter in the house, I having laid the same beside me for convenience sake.

"Hivers," I called out, "you needn't quat 'pon tap the butter if it be."

That turned his attention, and he got up, pretty smart, taking the best part o' the butter wi' un.

"These be only my workaday trousers, praise the Lord," he said.

I didn't make no commentary, being taken up wi' finishing the bread and bacon for fear lest worse might befall, but when that was put away I looked across at un—and zommat made me zay,—

" 'Tis a pity for you that Benjamin Parrot takes so long a-dying."

" Curse un and his money," said Martin, and wi' that he got up as if he would go, but I called un back from the door.

" Why," I said, " 'tis as like as not that the old man be worth thousands on thousands."

" Girt God Almighty—I'll not go nigh the maid," Martin cried, sort o' tremorful.

" There's more depends on your keeping away than you reckons on," I answered; which was true, though maybe not in the way he took it. When Martin was gone, I hiked straight off to the Common, and when I got full in the middle o' the green I zet to and laughed, but there was zommat queer about thic laugh, so that I was forced after a bit to give over and listen to the zound o' un. After thic I turned tail and erned *

* Ran.

back to the village as fast as my legs would
carry me. Toward the end o' the week
Martin begged a holiday from Farmer Burden and went to Barnstaple, a matter o' ten
miles by train from our village. The little
pea-green door o' Belle Hart's cottage was
on the latch, and the windys was all wide
open, because I went to zee, yet all that day
I felt sort o' suspicious. Then-all-to-wance
the idea comed over me to marry the maid
mezulf, and zay nought about it to no one,
for it zim'd her'd been talked about enough.
So the vallering night I dropped into her
cottage jest as it might be for a bit o' a tell.
I'd smartened mezulf up a bit, and my face
had a respectable shine on, for I hadn't
spared the soap. The maid was looking
wonderful purty, and her cheeks had a dash
o' colour in 'em that had been missing for
many a day. I hadn't thought out no special
plan, so I zot mezulf down, reckoning maybe
the wuds would come if I waited patient.
The village niver held me for good-looking,

though I reckon if I stood a bit higher in my shoes—I be just under five foot—there's more'n one o' the maids would ha' found me personable. I'd bought a new pair o' cords, and they gave out a fine, full-bodied crack each time I shifted in my chair. 'Twas a good thing I had 'em on, case they took it out o' the zilence and sort o' made conversation atween theirzulves.

"La! Zack," said Belle, arter a bit, "but you be dressed up wonderful smart."

"Tasty for the tasty," I answered, "and your looks become 'ee, ez they always do."

She gave a little snip o' a laugh. "So you think I'm looking well to-night?"

"Thet's zo."

She was zilent a bit, then-all-to-wance her tarned and laid a hand on my arm: "You be an old friend, Zack," her said, "and I know I can trust 'ee."

Law jay! thought I to mezulf, be her going to ax me or I her? Zo I nodded my

head and left it to my breeches to do the
friendly.

"I be a married woman, Zack," said she.

"Married!" said I.

"Ess, married," said she.

"Not married!" said I.

"Ess, married," said she.

"Good Gosh!" said I, "and who to?"

She bent down and sort o' whispered.
"Martin," says she. That was a bit too
much. Ever since the day Benjamin Parrot
had spoke o' leaving me his money I'd felt
so terrible alive, and now all to a sudden the
life was knocked clean out o' me. I reckon
Belle saw sommat in my face that scart her,
for she said, sort o' anxious,—

"You won't tell. Will 'ee, Zack?"

"Tell?" said I.

"You won't. Will 'ee?" says she.

"Tell!" said I.

"You won't, Zack. Will 'ee?" says she.

"Whativer should I tell for?" said I.

"I knowed I could trust 'ee," says she.

Then I found my feet and trapesed home,
and jest as I came nigh the door Farmer
Burden drove down the hill in his gig. He
pulled up when he saw me and bawled
acrass,—

"Benjamin Parrot's wuss, the dropsy's
started to mount."

I went into the house and slammed the
door in his face. The fire was out, so I zot
mezulf down afore a handful o' gray ash,
and the wind riz and hollered sort o' pain-
zome. I was niver no friend to wind, there's
zommat evil about un even when he purrs
zoft and makes as if he wudn't hurt 'ee for
the world; but this night, what wi' one
thing and t'other, the zound o' his voice
gived me the shudders.

"Tell," says I to mezulf, "o' course I
won't tell. Why should I tell?" And
the wind sort o' took the wuds up deri-
sive.

"No, you won't tell," says he. "You
know too much for thic."

"'Tis Martin's place to tell," says I. "Let um tell hiszulf."

"Martin mustn't tell," says the wind. "You'd lose the money then."

"The old man is dying," says I.

"Dying," bawled the wind—"dying."

"S'posing he died to-night," says I, "and niver knowed nought?"

"You'd git the money," says the wind thic terrible whispery that I fair shuddered at the sound o' the wuds. Then I tried to measure mezulf agin Martin, the zame maybe as the Almighty might be doing up above. I'd never broke no promise to the dead or drove my wife in zarrer to the grave. Minding on all the ill things Martin had done, I began to feel a bit more comfortable, for it zim'd as if the Lord must be on my side.

"Oh, o' course, He's on your side," says the wind.

There comed a banging great knock at the door, and I started fair to drop. I reckoned 'twas the Evil One hiszulf, though why iver

such an idea should crass my mind I can't
tell. I had forgot to fasten the catch, so
there was nought atween me and whoiver
'twas. Then the door opened and in walked
Martin. Hivers! I would 'most as soon it
had been the devil.

"Zack," says he, "they've sent for me
down to Parrot's. The old man's dying."

I didn't answer at all, and when Martin
saw that I hadn't wuds he walked over to
where I zot, and put one hand upon the
chimney-shelf, rested his face agin it and
gapnested down on the gray cinders.

"Dom Benjamin Parrot," he muttered,
sort o' slow. "Dom un."

"Be 'ee going?" I axed.

Martin tarned his great empty-zeeing
eyes on my face.

"What's the good?" he answered. "Me
and Belle was married the day afore last."

I hadn't nought to say, but the old clock
in the corner kept on bellowing "Wan minute less for Benjamin Parrot. Wan minute

less for Benjamin." All-to-wance Martin tarned as if he was about to be going, and at that zommat made me jump up and catch hold o' his arm.

" S'posing you don't tell," says I.

Martin gripped hold o' my arm thic hard I nigh hollered wi' the pain o' it.

" I've axed mezulf thic," he said.

My breath got that scart I was forced to zit down, for it zim'd to me that the devil wud ha' one or t'other o' us, and I prayed to God that it might be Martin.

" Zack," said he, " what wud it feel like to come by the money unhonest ? "

I kind o' crept togither. " Why do 'ee ax me thic, *now?* " I answered. But he didn't pay no speshil heed, and the clock hammered out so loud " Wan or t'other o' 'ee will have to pay for this," that I was certain sure Martin would hear and take heed in time. Instead o' thic he put his hand deep down in his pocket and pulled out a big canvas bag. Untying the string round the neck o' it, he poured a power o' gold and siller into his hand.

"It's took me all my life to save 'ut," he said, "and 'tiddn't a penny more than seven-and-seventy pun."

The sight o' the money sort o' hardened me. "Not much put aside o' Benjamin Parrot's," I answered.

"But it's come by honest," said Martin.

"'Tis only thieves and sich that harp so on baing honest," I tumm'l'd out. I couldn't abide the sound o' the wud on his lips thic often.

"Maybe," Martin answered, "for 'tis only since I thought o' baing a thief I've took to saying it."

Wi' that there riz up in my heart a banging great desire that he, not me, should try and steal the money dishonest, and I hungered after zommat temptatious to zay which hadn't no lie in it.

"Who'd be the loser s'posing you didn't tell?" I axed. Then I laughed out short and sharp, for I could answer that question better than he.

The wuds made Martin start. "S'posing I was to have a son," he said.

"You should think o' that afore you drow away the money—"

"I niver much keered to have childer," he said, half to hiszulf. "They eats up more'n they brings in most days, and a man be lucky when he comes to die if he has got enough together to pay for his own funeral and his wife's arter him, but s'posing so be that Belle bore me a son, I shud like un to be honest. I couldn't a-bear to blacken aught that comed to me droo her."

I sort o' hated the man. "Iddn't Benjamin Parrot dying while 'ee stand there and prate so purty about baing honest," I burst out. "And don't 'ee reckon to git the money if so be he shud die not knowing that you and Belle be man and wife."

"By the Lord," cried Martin, "I'll tell un the truth afore it be too late."

Then I saw what a vool I'd been to taun-
tify un, and I caught hold o' his arm.

"Bide where you be, the wuds wasn't
meant serious." He pushed me from un.

"I'll make no thief o' the child," he said.

The wuds had but jest crossed his lips
when a great solemnzome call-conscience
sound comed booming droo the house. Us
started one to t'other.

"You be too late," I said, "'tis the Passing Bell."

"The church clock is giving the hour,"
answered Martin, but I could zee the sweat
creep out upon his vace as us stood and
waited.

Zure enough there it comed again, two,
dree, four, vive, sax, seven, hate, nine, ten,
'leven, twalve. And wi' the last stroke
there fell sich a zilence as will drop upon
us, no doubt, at the last day when the Books
be opened and us harks to hear how all that
us have doed has looked in the eyes o' God
Almighty Hiszulf.

Standing there all o' a-listen, I didn't pay no more heed to Martin, for it zim'd to me that I stud afore the Jidgment Seat o' God and He kained down into my heart. I drapped on my knees and hid my vace afore Un. How long I kneeled there I can't tell, but when I comed to mezulf I was alone.

.   .   .   .

'Twas a week and a day after thic Benjamin Parrot died. Then it came out that he hadn't left no money, and the furniture had to be sold to pay for his funeral. Zim's twadn't nought but an annuity he had, arter all. He kind o' played wi' folks. "Human nater," he said, "was built for experimentation, and twadn't to be supposed that the Almighty should have all the pulling o' the strings to Hiszulf."

THE HALL AND HE

A HILL flung itself up, lazy fashion, behind Dunstable Weir, and from the top o' the same the Hall stared down on the village at its feet. Terrible, prosperous, big, the Hall looked, tiddleliwinkie the village, for the green fields, the trees that lolled above 'em and the stream that dippy-dappied through the meadowland was part o' the Hall; down in the village there was naught but ourselves and he. Two flights of steps led up to the Hall door, and then came wide waste places; I've tippy-toed through the same at times, and gapnested at the strange things upo' the wall, made believe to sit down upon the seats and open the doors that led into the rooms ayond, but that was when the squire and his daughter, Miss Elizabeth, were away in town, and no

45

one o' the great folk aside little Miss Bet
was at home. Half-way between the Hall
and the village stood the church, and there
it was that Miss Bet first clapped eyes on
he. The pew-backs were high in those days,
so that any other child who hadn't passed
her eighth year might have been put to
straits to see over them, but Miss Bet, hearing the scrape o' small feet in the pew behind, and having long been hard pressed for
companionship, had scant mind to be over-
come by the task. No one save the little
lady herself and the old squire were in the
Hall pew that Sunday morning, and he,
after casting one long look round the church
to see that we were all in our places, as it is
the duty of poor folk to be, sat himself
down in the big-cushioned seat and dropped
off to sleep amazing peaceful. Miss Bet
turned and eyed her grandfather—for such
the squire was—while from out the body of
the church, where the village was making
bold to re-cross its legs, there came a fine

shuffle and scrape. Taking heart at the
sound, maybe, the little lady sidled down
from her seat and began to gather the big
Bibles and pillar them one upon one till
they nigh topped the carved pew-back.
Then, without more ado, she mounted the
pile and stared down into a pair o' eyes as
black and determineful as her own. There
he sat, sure enough, a tall lath of a boy of
nine summers, puckered in between Aunt
Flint, who was housekeeper at the Hall in
those days, and a long tail of lower servants.
Many in the church besides Miss Bet wondered who the lad might be, the more, perhaps, because they marked how like the
lad's face was to her own. She had stared
but half her fill before the squire awoke, and,
squaring his elbows, upset the books on
which the young lady sat, so that she was
forced to a speedy quitting and us to wonder how she fared. Wi' the end o' the clatter
a fine silence fell upon the church. Parson
John looked over the rim o' the big leather

prayer-book sort o' questioning, and the
clerk stepped down to where we school
children sat by the altar rails, and knocked
our heads together two by two. He had
but jest got back to his seat, and Parson
John re-settled his spectacles, when a tiddleliwinkie sob came up from the bottom of the
squire's pew, and at that the lad was on his
legs and over the stout oak boards that
stood between him and the little lady in a
trice. We hadn't long to wait to see what
would happen after that, for no sooner was
he in the pew before the old squire took him
by the collar and pitched him fair back to
the place he had come from. Aunt Flint
was so scared that, not content to let him
bide, she up and re-sat him, terrible forcible,
in the self-same shiny spot. It was easy
seeing that the lad, for his part, was more
angered than shamed, and he thrust his lips
in upon his teeth, much after the fashion
of Miss Bet when she is wedded to aught
against her fancy.

My mother's habit on a Sunday afternoon was to step with me up to the Hall and take tea in the housekeeper's room. A pleasant habit enough I found it, for the room was lined with cupboards from top to bottom, and many taste-satious things were stored there in jars and boxes. Aunt Flint was a good ten years younger than my mother. A determineful spirit set in a thin wisp of a body, Aunt Flint did a power of ruling before she died. Ceremony was a thing she fancied, holding near kinship a scant excuse for lack of manners, and my mother, who was a comfortable, easy-natured woman, suffered a deal trying to act up to the same. At the last turn of the road leading to the Hall, my mother always stopped quat. "Now, Zack, lad," she would say, "don't let me take off my bonnet before your aunt has given me leave to untie the strings."

That afternoon she charged me more than once on the same matter, but my head being

full of the lad, I never gave thought to it till
I saw, by the tightening of Aunt Flint's lips,
that something had gone amiss.

"La, Jane," my mother burst out, "if I
haven't taken off my bonnet unbeknown to
myself. I know 'tis over familiar, but there!
a person's hands goes up unconscious to the
strings, more particularly if the day is hot
and they are short-necked, the same as myself."

Now if there was one thing that my aunt
disliked more than the clipping back of ceremony, it was what she called over-wordiness;
my mother, knowing this well, would will-
ingly have bided silent had it but been possible for one of her nature to do so. "Give
me a dumb man to one whose tongue is too
near speech," was a saying of Aunt Flint's,
but to-day she closed her lips tight over her
thoughts. For my part, I was all agog to
see the lad once again, but the room was
bare of him, and my eyes strayed to the window. Below, squared in by tall box hedges,

was Miss Elizabeth's garden, and from where
I sat I could see Miss Elizabeth herself pak-
ing slowly to and fro. Tall she was and
dark, the same as the old squire and Master
Geoffry, Miss Bet's father, who was away
in India soldiering. Her hands hung sort o'
listless, so did her head, and her dress sulked
behind her over the grass, looking marvellous white against the green. Miss Bet shot
past unmarked, then, all at once, the lad
came full rush from among the trees. At
the sight of him the lady stopped short and
thrust out her hands as if to push him from
her, but he stood his ground, looking into
the face of her sort o' proud and abashed to
one. Being but a chink of a child at the
time, I felt afear'd for him, and would have
called to the lad to come away had I dared
to bring notice on myself. However, after a
bit, Miss Elizabeth turned and trailed away,
and he bided where he was.

"God sakes, Jane!" said my mother, "if
they two aren't as like one t'other as leaves

from the same book. No wonder you tell me there is blood in him. Souls and bodies," she clattered on, "don't look at me the like o' that, Aunt Flint, and you but just telling me I must take the lad back home wi' me and treat him for all the world the same as little Zack here."

Aunt Flint pressed one black mittened hand 'pon top the other. "And isn't Zack your son?"

"La, yes," my mother answered, "and familiar as such from a child."

"Well, treat them same for same."

At that my mother fell silent for a bit. "Zack 'ull have to work for his living wi' his hands," she said.

"Ah!" answered Aunt Flint, slowly, "that's where blood tells."

Then the lad came in and my mother made ready to go, kaining across at him, half suspicious, half friendly to one. He must have been pillared and posted a deal in his bit of a life, for he took it all wonderful unconcerned, reckoning mayhap that one home was like to be as good as another. We started at a slow pace, my mother having a fancy for being smaller-footed than she, in fact, was, went tender in her best boots. Not that she ever allowed such to be the case, holding rather that it was the shortness of her neck that stood her enemy. Our cottage sat square in a hollow, wi' three wind-twisted fir trees standing out on the hill's edge above. It was cob-walled and had four windows to the front and two to the back, the door being poked away at the side. A red brick path ran round the house, shooting out a long arm between the same and the gate. Flowers there were in plenty and no poor show o' beans and taties. Over the door was a big white-faced clock, the hands pointing to half after noon. My father was a watchmaker by trade and more than usual inventive, so that nothing which might perchance go by wheel but was forced, sooner or later, to make the attempt. On that score he and my mother were by no means of one mind, for, as she said, "He took the familiar off things till she was fair scared o' the place."

The sun had just tipped the hill when we reached the three firs, and my mother, having undone the strings of her bonnet, peered down upon our cottage to see if all had gone well in her absence. A fine chime o' laughter slapped up from below.

"Why, Zack," she said, "whativer be all the folk gaping at?" I moved a few paces nearer. "'Tis some o' your father's inventive tricks, you may be bound," she called after me. Two black things, that looked more like vegetable marrows than aught else, were running along the red brick path at a most amazing rate. "Hurry," cried my mother, "and see what 'tis."

"Naught but your old house boots on wheels," I bawled back.

At that my mother was on her feet and

after me, skidding over the ground with a fine contempt for the stones.

"Bodies and souls," she cried, "if I didn't reckon to have hidden they boots safe from un in the stick-rick."

"Off wi' they tight-wasted shoes o' yours, Martha," said my father as she came square upon him through the gate.

"Oh, you Sabbath-breaker," she answered. "You idle hands beloved o' Satan!"

"Come, come," he said, "'tis but the boots in search for the woman, in place o' the woman in search o' the boots. I dare swear you'll be glad enough to get they poor swollen feet o' yours into zommat more sizeable."

All this time the boots themselves were click-clacking up and down the path, and my mother, out o' breath and out o' pride, burst into tears at the sight o' 'em. The neighbours who had been standing by, well pleased wi' the sport, slunk away one by one, leaving father looking over the tops of his spectacles at my mother.

"Why, Martha," he said, "you ain't pleased after all!" Once started to cry, my mother sobbed away right lustily, and it was long before words came to her again.

"How often shall I be forced to tell 'ee, Ebenezer," she said, "that I can't abide the inventive; but there, 'tis just like 'ee to shame me afore the lad—and this the first time he has ever set eyes on the house."

"What lad be thic?"

"Why, *he*, o' course," she answered, kaining round in search of him.

But he wasn't there.

Later, when my mother had dried her eyes and was busy laying supper, he came and knocked at the door of the cottage—and I reckon of my mother's heart as well.

He and the village never took to one another; this did not surprise my mother, but I think she was a bit put out at his not being friends with his book. Learn he either couldn't or wouldn't, and he and the cane got close acquainted. My mother used to

argue wi' him sometimes when she bound up
his hands in a bit of damp rag after a more
than usual bad basting, but, though he was
fonder o' her than of any, save one, she
couldn't get him to mend his ways.

" And well I know," she would mutter to
herself as she tucked him into bed after having her say out—" that 'tis naught but the
blood, Latin would be pap to 'ee." Every
Sunday, wet or dry, mother took both us
lads to the Hall. I was forced to bide 'long
'o her and Aunt Flint, but they let him play
in the rose garden that spread out in front o'
Miss Elizabeth's windows, and if the little
lady chanced to be with her aunt at those
times, she would come scurrying down to
him, for he and Miss Bet had always a deal
to tell one another.

Just as he entered his fourteenth year, a
hurrying sickness fell upon the village, so
that the folks were no sooner ill than dead.
Rich and poor it treated with an equal hand,
paying no more heed to the quality than if

they were born simple, and on that score many called it the Leveller. 'Twas midsummer, and the night Miss Elizabeth was struck down wi' it, the hot air had dried the marrow o' sleep out o' me, so that I couldn't rest, do what I would. All to once the door opened and I closed my eyes, because it was a habit of mother's to up with a lad's shirt and slipper him if his eyes weren't fast buttoned afore the clock struck ten. She tippy-toed across, shading the light back wi' her hand, and the utmost end o' me tweaked from sheer nervousness o' what might soon be laid upon it, but she passed by my bed and went over to where the lad was sleeping sound enough. There she stood an amazing long time, muttering to herself—"Bodies and souls." Then the door opened again and Aunt Flint came in. I knew who 'twas because one o' her legs is shorter than t'other, which makes her go dappy.

" 'Tis flinging the child's life after a dead

one; for Miss Elizabeth is as good as parted," said my mother.

" The child's her child."

" More shame at the sacrifice."

" Come," exclaimed my aunt, sharply, " wake the lad ; the sooner he is dressed the better."

"She has lived wi'out un, let her die wi'out un," my mother answered harshly.

" If she hadn't done the first, maybe she could have foregone the last," said my aunt, and at that mother gave in.

" Ay," she murmured, " if us had but strength to do right in this life, but us haven't; there's times when we must fail, every mother's son o' us. Oh, bodies and souls, bodies and souls, 'twud be well if we were all one or all t'other."

" Don't waste time blaspheming," Aunt Flint put in harshly. " Be thankful that, if mixed we are, the mixing was done by higher hands than ours."

" And they but 'prentice, with all reverence be it spoke," said my mother. At that, feeling perhaps that she had been a bit free, seeing who it was she had been criticising, she made haste to wake and dress the lad.

When the room was bare of him and Aunt Flint, and naught but a great streak of moonlight across the bed where he had lain, my mother knelt down beside it, and, covering her face with her worn, red hands, burst into tears.

" Oh, God Almighty ! " she sobbed, " you put us into this world and gave us hearts to love wi' and childer to love, don't take 'em from us when once they be given, but be content to let 'em bide well placed."

After a bit she rose and stole away, shutting the door behind her, and leaving me to wonder whether 'twas for the sparing o' the lad's or my life her was praying so mortal fervent—and in either case what was like to befall. The next morning when I woke he was back in bed and sleeping sound. I peered across at him, and thought to myself

that his hair had grown terrible black all to
once, maybe though that his face was whiter
than it was wont. Then my mother came
and whipped me off to the kitchen, telling
me to dress and leave the lad undisturbed.
That day week Miss Elizabeth was buried.
The rain fell and fell, so that the quality
could scarce be seen behind the carriage
windows, but as the long list o' them slurred
down the hillside, the lad shot out from behind an elm, put himself straight behind the
hearse and walked chief sorrower afore 'em
all. Some were for stopping and laying a
whip across his back, but most said : " Who
be he ? No one will mark sich for the rain."
So they let him bide, and when the coffin
was lowered, the earth thrown in, and the
gentry shut tight and dry inside their carriages, he flung himself 'pon top the grave.
I wondered why he sorrowed, seeing that she
had never loved him. The lad fell ill later,
and mother packed me off to live wi' Aunt
Flax, a sister o' my father's on the far side

o' the hill, where food was scarce and hands heavy, so that I was glad enough to look home in the face again five weeks later. It seemed most as if the lad had spent every moment of they long five weeks in growing, for he was shot up tall enough to stand shoulder to shoulder wi' my father. I marked, too, that he was more concerned wi' his own thoughts than ever, though I had always held him for silent. Still, outside my mother, speech wasn't much in the family, so that he and me were well content to bide unquestioned the one o' the other. Aunt Flint was dead, the levelling sickness having gripped her the same night Miss Elizabeth was taken ill o' it. She nursed her lady to the last, and, when all was over save the burying, went upstairs, lay down 'pon top the bed and died, quick and quiet, alone to herself. The keys o' the cupboards and a recipe for the making o' ketchup, for which she had been held in much honour during life, were on the table

at her elbow; also, they say, a few lines in
pencil to put 'em in mind that the morrow
was the day for cleaning out the kitchen
flue. We missed Aunt Flint regular tea-
time Sundays, for a new housekeeper had
come to the Hall, and me and the lad never
went there as we'd been wont, but were
forced to lie in the fields and talk o' the tall
oak cupboards set deep in the wall, wi' the
rows and rows o' boxes and jars o' sweet
things inside o' 'em. I reckon, though I
never heard mother make mention o' the
matter, that the money for the lad's keep
stopped quat wi' Miss Elizabeth's death.
Let that be as it may, I know it was just
about that time there was talk o' putting the
lad to a trade, but he hadn't no talent for
fancying such out for hisself, and mother
was all for letting him bide his time. "Far
be it from me to presume wi' the quality,"
she said. "Let him be, and the blood will
forrard un better than iver we can." So he
was let bide.

It was a long time now since the lad had
had speech wi' Miss Bet, and I reckon
maybe he missed the same, for one Sunday
when the service was over he didn't bide in
his place till after the squire and the little
lady had left the church, as is customary for
all o' us to do, but up and marched out
straight at their heels. The old squire, hearing the clump-clump after him—for the lad's
boots were a size or so too big, to allow his
feet to spread—turned round, and the lad
looked up in his face.

"I want," he said, "to walk home wi' Bet."

At that the squire's red face grew a bit
redder and a grim kind o' smile came upon
the same.

"Well, Bet," he called out in his big voice,
"what answer am I to make to your cava-
lier?"

"I like him," said the little lady, for she
was never one to desert a friend.

"Then be off with you both," the squire
answered.

But the following day he rode down and
said that such a thing must not happen
a second time, and my father passed his
word that it should not.

The old squire never wasted wonder as
to who the lad might be, for all that he
was featured marvellous after the family
pattern. Mayhap he did not chance upon
the likeness, or, if he did, reckoned wi'
the village that Master Geoffry had been a
bit over-zealous wi' one o' our wenches, for
the lad, from the wearing o' yokel's boots,
had got the yokel's tread, and seemed to me
nearer o' kin to us than he had first-along.
In my mother's eyes, howsoever, he was always Miss Elizabeth's son, a gentleman, and,
maybe, though he never put tongue to the
words, he saw at one with her in the matter.
Whiles I used to wonder if he was always
going to bide content 'long o' us. I reckon,
though, 'twas my mother who worried most
over such, dearly wishful o' keeping him to
herself and yet all o' a hunger to see him

taking his rightful place afore the world.
The lad's birthday fell on the edge o' spring,
and the morning o' his seventeenth year
mother awoke us early, and, giving each
a hunk o' bread and bacon, told us to be off
to the woods to gather in an appetite for
dinner. For a while we lay under the
chestnut trees marking the buds bursting
out o' their coats, and sporting, terrible
green, twisty and pleased, wi'out 'em. Then,
all to once, up us sprang and ran as if the
devil himself was at our tail till we got to
the brook, and the lad was all for jumping
it, though it was a good eighteen foot from
bank to bank and uncommon deep on the far
side. Jump he did, and in he fell. After a
deal o' gurgling and splashing, he got hold
o' the bough o' a willow, and was pulling
himself up the bank by aid o' it, when who
should peer down through the branches but
Miss Bet. Now, the little lady had been
absent from the Hall a year or more, and
had grown most 'mazing pleasant to look on,

so that the sight o' her put all thought
o' where he was out o' the lad's mind, being
all eyes and gapnest, till the willow twig,
snapping in two, souse he went under the
water again. At that Miss Bet burst into
such a chime o' laughter that he was forced
by anger and shame to find a speedy footing,
which he did, and in a twinkling was off out
of view.

"Why," cried Miss Bet, "the big booby
has run away."

"'Tis his birthday, and mother said he
was sure to be home in good time for
dinner," I answered, a bit vexed that
the mere sight o' the little lady's face
should make such hay o' a lad's wits, for
I could not but remember I was a lad myself.

"Is he as greedy as all that?" she asked,
opening her eyes wide.

I turned my back on her and hiked off
home, for I was never an admirer of women's
clack. He was lying at the foot of the three

wind-twisted firs, and raised his head as I came by.

" Well," I burst out, flinging myself down beside him, " of all the gabies— " but he cut me short.

" Did you see her ? " he asked.

" Yes, and heard, too. I reckon she's laughing at us still." The blood struck across his face and those black eyes o' his looked terrible big and bright.

" You didn't see her near the same as I did," he said.

" No, and glad enough I am not to have, for a more sorry figure than you made 'twud be hard to cut."

" Oh," he said, flinging back his head, " you never saw her, 'twadn't possible from where you stood— "

" Let us get back home to dinner," I answered, for I was sick o' talk just then.

He rose terrible reluctant, stretched his arms and drew in a mighty big breath. " A lad makes but a poor show afore a maid," he said.

"More especially if he has had his fill o' muddy water," I answered.

At that he started down the hill at a fine pace, seeming most as anxious to be home to dinner as I was myself, but when once the victuals was afore him, not a mouthful would he touch, till my mother was near crying wi' vexation. Nothing would satisfy her short o' hearing the full tale of our doing that morning, and when I told her what had passed she grew terrible silent all-to-once and would have forgot to give me a third helping o' pudding if I hadn't made believe to have cut my finger. Then she comed to herself, and, having scolded me roundly, heaped up the plate more than usual high, so that after disposing of the same I was glad to stretch myself out under one of the apple trees and sleep. The lad kept solitary company the next few days, being up and out wi' the first creeping in of dawn and

biding away till nightfall. When I asked
him where he had been, he answered, "Nowhere in particular," so that I was forced
to track out his way for myself. That day,
however, he didn't go no further than the
brook, and there he lay kaining across at the
big willow where the little lady had sat and
laughed on the morning he fell into the
water.

It seemed to be but a poor fashion of passing the time, gapnesting across at an old willow tree, and I would ha' left him if the little lady had not chosen just that moment to
trip out from the woods and along the bank
over-agin where we lay. At sight o' her the
lad sprang to his feet and pulled off his cap.

"Dear me, are you really dry again?" she
called across.

"'Tis naught o' a jump," he answered, the
blood aflame in his face.

"Indeed!"

"Leastways, I could jump it to-day," he
said.

" Why to-day ? "

" I could jump it to-day," he repeated, stubbornful.

" Please don't try, you will only fall in, and I am sure you can't afford to spoil your clothes," she cried, seeing him run back a few steps ; but wi' a rush and a spring he was over at her side.

" There," he said, " I knowed I could do it to-day."

" Why to-day ? " she asked, curious-like.

" Becase," he tummil'd out, speaking terrible broad—for, wi' all his blood, he had grown at one wi' us in speech—" becase you be over to here."

I reckon myself that Miss Bet was a bit taken aback at this speech o' the lad's, for she was silent a while, then she asked all-to-once, " Where's little Zack ? "

Now, though I bain't as big, I be full as old as the lad hisself, so I wasn't altogether made up in being spoken of as " little Zack," but that is neither here nor there.

"I dunno," he answered.

"Perhaps he is at the fair?"

"Maybe."

"He works for Farmer Burden, doesn't he?"

"Ess."

"And you?"

"I don't go to work."

"Why not?"

"I dunno," he said, sullenful.

She looked him up and down. "But surely," she asked, "a big fellow like you are is not content to be idle all day?"

He didn't make no answer.

A bit of a smile crept into her face. "Perhaps you mean to earn a living by your head and not with your hands. That is what all you young men do nowadays, isn't it?" she asked.

He turned and walked a few paces from her. "I ain't larned," he said. At that she seemed a bit sorry to have spoke.

"Well," she said, going up to him and

touching his arm, "I am glad to have seen
you again. Do you remember we used to
play together as children ? "

He didn't answer her a word, but stood
there terrible proud and downcast to one.
The little lady looked at him a moment and
then began to move slowly away.

" Good-bye," she said, stopping and kain·
ing back at him, but he made as if he hadn't
heard, so she walked on and left him. When
there wasn't no sound o' her footsteps nor no
sight o' her atween the trees, he flung hisself
down 'pon top the earth and sobbed and
sobbed. I couldn't mind that I had ever
seen him do the like afore, and I wondered
what 'twas that made un do it then. He
didn't come home to supper that night, and
it seemed to me that the next few days
mother was as much put about as he was,
and glad enough I felt when Sunday came
round and there was a chance o' a hot dinner
making us all feel much more ourselves ; but
the lad seemed fixed to being contrary, and

sat staring down at his victuals, for all the
world as if they was a photographing ma-
chine and he a-wait for the canary. It angered me only to see him, and when, to make
matters worse, mother got up from the table
afore the meal was half over and shut herself into the back kitchen, I jest sat down in
front o' the pudding and did duty for they
that had no appetite. Father looked over
his spectacles at me, much as if he were wondering if so be I were mother or no, then
afore he had quite come to one mind on the
matter, he fell back into thought o' other
things. He and me went to afternoon service alone that day, and when us comed
home mother and the lad was sitting hand
in hand before the fire. Tea was laid, and
she fetched the kettle off the hob and soon
we were all seated round the table, each o'
us silent, saving mother, who was painful
silent. After a bit the lad rose up and
stole out. When the door had shut ahind
him mother looked across at father. "He

iddn't going to bide here no longer," she said.

"Who iddn't?" asked my father in his dreadful voice.

"The lad," she answered wi' a catch in her throat.

"Oh," said my father, and fell back to dreaming once more. After a bit mother looked up a second time. "He iddn't going to bide here no longer," she said.

"Who iddn't?" asked my father once again.

"The lad," she answered.

"Dear me," said my father, "is that so—"

"Yes," she answered, "he iddn't going to bide here no longer."

"Who?—Yes, I mind who you be talking o'—the lad—ah, dear me," said my father.

"'Twill be lonesome wi'out un," she murmured.

There wasn't no answer.

" 'Twill be lonesome wi'out un," she said again.

" What's that you say ? " asked my father, waking up from his thoughts.

" 'Twill be lonesome wi'out un," she re-peated.

" Wi'out un ?—Yes, I mind who you mean —the lad—so 'twill—dear me—so 'twill— very lonesome—"

" He's going to work for hisself—earn his own living," she said.

" Is that so ? " my father answered.

" He'll be back among his own afore long, mark me if he isn't, ' she said.

" Yes."

" I knowed from the fust he wouldn't bide content along o' us—"

" Yes," said my father, getting a bit dream-ful once more.

" The blood won't let un bide content; like to like."

There wasn't no answer.

" Dree years he'll bide from us—"

Father didn't hear naught o' what her was talking about.

"I shall think o' un most days," she said, rising and kaining round, first at father, then me, and last of all at the lad's empty chair. "'Twill be lonesome wi'out," she ended up, "lonesomer than afore he comed."

The night before he went mother packed his clothes in a wooden box afore the kitchen fire. A wonderful lot o' extries she put in, lest at some time he might be in need and not have, nor did she forget to tuck a big bottle o' Aunt Flint's ketchup deep down in the corner o' the box, and which the lad told me afterwards was so ill-fated as to break on the way, making a terrible varigationny among his shirts. The lad hisself sat on the edge o' the table and watched the packing, mother keeping me on the trot fetching odds and ends. A deal o' good advice she put in 'long o' the clothes, and the lad listened 'mazing attentive to all she had to say, though I reckon his mind

wasn't all wi' her. Maybe she thought the
same, for, after a bit, she gave over speech
and packed away continuous, saving that
every now and a while she would stop and
rub the back o' her hand sort o' unsuspicious across her eyes. At that the lad
edged hisself along the table till he was
over-agin where she stood, and kained into
her face, so that she was forced to either
turn her back or let him see that she was
crying.

" 'Tis wearisome work for 'ee, lad, this
over-telling," she said, raising her face to his,
and he, ruckying down, kissed a kink in her
chestnut hair ; she was comely to look on
was my mother.

" Your hair do grow mortal tasty on your
head, mother," he answered, randomlike.

She put up her hands and patted her hair.
" It hasn't the colour it had once," she said,
sort o' contemptuous.

" Why," he asked, " twadn't iver more
takeful looking than 'tis now, surely ? "

"Ah, that it was," she answered, all o' a smile to be put in mind o' they days.

"Do you hear what mother be telling, Zack?" he asked, turning round my way.

"I've heard father say the same many a time," I answered.

"Well, well," said the lad, "and the men came courting 'ee, I s'pose, mother?"

"There was never no lack o' they," she answered, getting back to contempt.

"You led 'em a fine dance, I dare swear," he said.

"I didn't favour 'em, a man favoured is a man lost."

"How did 'ee come to a choice at last, mother?" he asked, they black eyes o' his all o' a twinkle.

"Well," she answered, "I can't rightly say, 'less 'twas I took the one that was the most aggravating, for aggravating he was, and a more inventuous man never walked between leather."

At that moment my father came in carrying something in his hand. "I was just saying, Ebenezer," she added, nodding across at him, "that you was always a terrible aggravating man."

He smiled kind o' simple. "I've got a little sommat here that I thought might be useful to the lad, seeing that he is going to furren parts."

"Bodies and souls o' us, what is it?" mother asked, leaning forward. "I suspicioned well that you was at the inventive, for not a wink did you sleep last night, or let anyone else sleep either."

Drawing a chair a bit away from the rest o' us, my father sat hisself down. " 'Tis simple and yet 'tis cunning," he said. "Taken to pieces 'tiddn't much more than two pieces o' elastic."

"Some o' us 'ull live to regret it for all that," my mother put in.

" 'Tis wonderful ingenious to look on," the lad said, "and I should dearly like to know what 'tis for."

"For keeping your trousers out o' the mud."

At that mother relented a bit. "'Tis a good end in view anyway," she said.

"Well," put in the lad, "but I be curious to know how it works."

My father got up from his chair and walked across to him. "I reckon there iddn't another man in the parish that could have invented its like," he said, not without pride. "'Tis worn above the knee, so," he added, fixing the skiddick as he spoke.

"Be it on?" asked my mother.

"Yes."

"Why, his trousers look for all the same as they did afore."

"That's becase I've set it for fine weather."

"Law!" exclaimed mother, crossly, "what are we all here for?"

At that the lad's trousers seemed to get a bit flurried and started to roll theirselves up mortal ingenious. When they reached the knee, he looked across at my father and then down at his bare shins sort o' questionful.

"See 'em work, jest see 'em work," cried my father, clapping hands. "I reckon Exeter mud 'ull not touch un wi' the likes o' they on his legs."

The rest o' us held silent, part from surprise and part becase we weren't sure if worse would befall the lad, but the trousers, having twisted theirselves well round the knees, seemed content to bide there.

"Unroll 'em for the lad's sake," said my mother.

"He'll have to wait till he takes 'em off to do that," father answered.

The baker had promised to gi' the lad a lift to the station in his cart. When he came round the next morning, and the box was hoisted into place and the lad had his foot on the step, mother, who had been wonderful talkative all the morning, walked into the house wi'out a word, so that he went unsped, saving for myself, becase

father, having lit on a marvellous taking
notion for the making o' pavement out o'
cork, had forgotten about his going altogether. As for the lad, he cried open
through the village, though he was dry-eyed
enough when the cart left our door. I
couldn't but think that if I had been he I
would have taken care to do my crying at
home. Saving that he would be back in a
year, he hadn't let on naught o' where he
was minded to go, but we reckoned he
wouldn't come back wi'out seeing Exeter.
Eight and threepence was tied up in the
corner o' his handkerchief, which was all the
money there was in the house at the time o'
his going.

"He'll see travel wi' that," mother said;
"the blood hasn't stirred him for naught."

"Maybe he'll get eddicated," I put in, becase I couldn't but hold it a pity that he
spoke so terrible different from Miss Bet.

My mother tossed her head at that. "Eddication is all very well for the likes o' us,"

she answered, "but a gentleman can do wi'out it."

"Do 'ee reckon that he'll ever be a gentleman again?" I asked.

"He'll take his place," she answered; "a gentleman he is and always will be."

Mother was never over fond of using her feet, but most evenings after the lad had left us she would climb the hill to the three wind-twisted firs above our house and kain across at the Hall windies. She said that the sight o' 'em brought the lad nearer. Whiles she would have me go wi' her, part because I was a prop to lean on, and more, maybe, that, having a tongue, she dearly liked a tell. One after t'other the lights would spring up in the windies, only Miss Elizabeth's wing would bide black and desartful, gapnesting sort o' dead-eyed down on the long rose garden where the lad played as a child. Towards they 'twas that my mother kained. "Over to there he was born," she told me once, nodding her head

that ways, "though none outside your Aunt
Flint knowed o' the same. 'Twas on midsummer night that he comed into the world,
and her mopped un 'round in a big Indie
shawl and carried un down to this very
identical spot where you and I be sitting."

"Hivers, mother," I tummil'd out, "and
what happened to him then?"

"Your father took un from her. Dree
full days Ebenezer was absent, and where
he went is unbeknown to me," she answered;
"for your father is a secret man when he is
so minded, though, maybe, you never gave
him credit for it. Your Aunt Flint put
more trust in him than she did in me, for all
I was own sister to her and zeed the world
for ten full years afore she was born.
Not," my mother added, "that I ever held
her for wrong in doing the same, for I
always say a secret is best kept by the
man that doesn't know it."

"Who was the lad's father?" I asked,
after a bit.

She fell silent a long while afore answering, " Did 'ee ever hear tell o' Black Mark Hay o' Chickenham Chase ? " she said.

" He that shot himself ? "

" The same."

" Surely 'twas Black Mark the old squire threw down the Hall steps."

" Ay ; and 'tis told that Miss Elizabeth followed un out and gave herself to un thic same night."

" And then ? " I asked.

" He shot himself.   Reckoning to have a sure revenge on the squire.   But the squire never larned the truth.   No, nor ever will."

I turned my eyes from the Hall, that stood so banging big and alone a-top the hill to kain down on our cottage.

" And does the lad know ? " I said, after a bit.

" Yes, Miss Elizabeth told un the night she died."

" It must ha' been hard for her to find words," I said.

"Her had been fifteen long years looking for 'em," my mother answered, "and when it comed to the last, they was still to seek. Her lay and kained at the lad, and he, but half-fared back from sleep, kained back at her. Her held out her hands, but he did not stir. Then she cried out fierce to Aunt Flint, 'Why doesn't he come to me?' And your Aunt Flint said, 'He is afear'd to come.' 'No,' she cried back, ''tis I that be afear'd.' And at that the lad stepped forwards. 'I bain't afear'd,' said he. 'What be it?' 'Come nearer,' she said; and he came nearer. 'Give me your hand,' she said; and he gave her his hand. 'Stoop down,' she said; and he stooped down. 'Lay your face on mine,' she said; and he did as she bade un, so that the tears that fell from her eyes fell 'pon him. Then he raised his head and looked her full in the face. 'Be you my mother?' he asked. And she answered 'Yes,' and wi' that she died."

The wind twisted droo the firs above our heads kind o' forlorn, and it seemed a forlorn tale. I sprang up and shook myself. "Let us be gitting home along, mother," I said.

"There be no getting home for the lad," she muttered, rising as I bade her. "Ah, bodies and souls—bodies and souls—one may know what 'tis to be lonesome, but that don't make one better able to save they one loves from the same." Then us went down the hill, slow as us had climbed up, for 'twas dark, the moon not having riz, and naught hurt mother more than to put her foot on a loose stone unexpected.

Us never got no letters from him, but then he was but a poor hand wi' his pen. I said to mother, "He's quality—why don't he learn to write?"

"Such things come natural to the quality —when they ha' need o' 'em," she answered.

"'Tis my belief 'twill never come natural to he," I returned.

"And what if so be it don't?" she said
hotly. "Is he the less quality for all o'
that?"

"Well, if you be content, and the lad be
content, I don't see it much matters any-
how," I answered.

My mother nodded knowingful. "Jest
you wait till he comes back, and, mark me,
but you'll see a mighty big difference in un."

"Why," I asked, "do you reckon he'll
have got eddication?"

"Eddication," she repeated scornfully;
"ay, and a deal aside thic. Who knows but
that he is with the quality at this very
minute?"

I bided silent after that, for if such was
the case I didn't wish to be the one to speak
lightly o' un.

Twasn't so very long after the lad left
us before the Hall stood empty—the squire
and Miss Bet being away in furren parts.
Mother said 'twas as it should be. "For
why," she asked, "should they be there

when he wasn't?" Seemed to me that she spoke a little too free o' the squire in those days, finding his ways cheap set aside those o' the lad. Still, if it so happened that the squire rode past our door and stopped to speak to her, she was all o' a fluster o' curt-seys, and would say afterwards that "A button o' the quality's was worth the coat o' your new-made man." Father wasn't quite at one wi' her on this score, holding respect too finedacious to be set altogether aside for the quality. But mother would answer, "You can but respect they you were born to respect."

"Ay, ay," father would agree, and go off nodding his head, leaving mother a bit per-plexed, for she could never tell for certain at the end o' the argufication whether father sided wi' her or no.

The night before the lad's return the squire and Miss Bet came back to the Hall, and mother climbed up to the three firs to look at the lit-up windies, for she said,

"Who can tell but the lad himself might not be behind one o' 'em?" And the thought o' such made her angered and pleased, sorry and contentful to one.

" 'Twon't be long afore he's down here, if so be he is up to the Hall," she said, and then broke off to mutter to herself, "I reckon he iddn't there, 'tis home he wud come fust along. Maybe 'tiddn't more than jest to welcome un the squire's back for."

I cudn't but reckon the old squire had come to the Hall for other than that, though I didn't say so, because a year be a long time, and the wisest o' us can't say all that 'ull happen in it. Besides, there wasn't no doubt but that the lad had been born quality. A deal o' baking mother did on the strength o' the lad's coming, so that the house fair smelt o' the hot oven. When dinner was over and the afternoon began to wear on, mother put father's tools away, and, fetching his best coat, she locked him and it together into the spare attic, having made up her mind to be quit o' the inventive for this one afternoon. That done, she sent me to climb one o' the three firs to keep a good lookout for the lad, while she herself stood at a little wicket gate ready to welcome him.

"Mind," she said, as I started to do as I was bid, "you are to keep one eye on the Hall and t'other on the village."

Howsomever, I reckoned that it was from the village he would come, and that way I kept my face turned. A 'mazing time I waited, but, jest as dimmet began to fall, I saw a long-legged lad that might ha' been he, saving there wasn't no quality-look about un whatsoiver.

"Hi, mother!" I bawled out, "there's a lad, but no ginelman, coming village-ways."

Her made as if her hadn't heard, but I could see that her was a bit flusticated, be-cause her twisted her apron round from front to back.

All the while the lad, if so be 'twas he, was coming nearer.

"Hi, mother!" I bawled out a second time, "for sartin 'tiddn't no ginelman."

By that her had caught sight o' the lad herself, for he 'twas, sure enough. Her gave one screech, and I near falled out o' the tree at the sound o' it, and then off her went down the hill, like a hen after her chickens, and was kissing and sobbing over un, till I thought to myself that I was glad enough 'twas he and not me who had been away from home. I got down slow enough, for I wasn't going to hurry myself, seeing that a year hadn't made no such 'mazing difference in the looks o' un.

"Be that 'ee, Zack?" he cried out.

"Why, you've got the same clothes on that you went away in," I answered.

Then we went in, mother unlocked father, and we all sat down to tea. Glad enough I was that the coming home of one meant extra meat-times to those that had bided be-

hind. Father had got thic knotted up in
thought from having been left so long to
hisself that tea was half over afore he
marked the lad was present. Pleased
enough he was to do him welcome, and
when I leaned across the table and whispered, "He hasn't prospered none," I thought
father must ha' mistook my meaning, for
he acted for all the world as if that stood to
the lad's credit. I could not but be mortal
curious to larn what the lad had been up to
all that long year, but he was silent consarn-
ing it, and mother wouldn't ha' him pressed,
though, after a bit, it leaked out that he
had been to Exeter, and as much was made
o' that as if he had seen the Queen. His
hands were terrible rough and worn away,
and when I asked how that had comed about,
he said he had been hod-boy to a mason.

"Hivers!" cried I, "there wasn't no
need to go all the way to Exeter to larn
that trade."

And he answered 'twas the only work he

could get. I thought to myself that if I had been he I would ha' kept that quiet, seeing as how he was quality and had gone off that fanfarish. Wi' the setting in o' dimmet he stole away by hisself, and I found un later beneath the fir trees, kaining across at the Hall. I felt a bit sorry for un.

"You would like to be living over along wi' they?" I said.

He didn't make no answer for a while, but tarned those black eyes o' his on me sort o' questionful. "I bain't but jest come home," he said.

"Why don't 'ee larn to speak more like ginelfolks, seeing that you are quality?" I tummil'd out, for the clack o' his tongue always kind o' tarned me agin un.

He reddened up at that, and then he said, sort o' wistful, "Do 'ee reckon, Zack, Miss Bet would lay my speech agin me?"

"Miss Bet," I answered, "don't trouble her head over such, seeing that she holds you for naught above the hod-boy that you be."

The blood crept away from un, leaving his face white, but he didn't say naught, and I felt kind o' sorry for un again.

"If so be you was to tell her who by rights you are," I put in, after a bit, "she might help you back to yourself."

"I sha'n't niver get back to myself thic ways," he answered.

"Nor no ways," I said short; "for you ain't got it in 'ee."

'Twas about a week after that he and me was standing under they same fir trees, when who should ride down the hill but the little lady, for 'mazing small she was in spite o' being on the way to seventeen summers. The lad rose to his feet and stood sort o' tremorful, and she pulled up 'longside o' us.

"Why, Zack," she said, "is that you?" but she looked at the lad as she spoke.

"You be still the little lady, I see, Miss Bet, for all the furren air you have drank in," I answered.

At that she broke into one o' her chimes

o' laughter. "Don't quiz me, Zack. You are none too big yourself—remember."

"Lads grow and maids don't," I said, for I never could abide being held for small.

" Oh," she answered, " I shall trust in Providence," and then, wi' a nod to us both, she rode on her way.

When she was fair out o' sight, I turned to the lad. " You were 'mazing silent, considering you hold such a deal by the 'pinion o' Miss Bet," I said.

But he kained down the bare hill track. " Did 'ee see her, Zack ? " he asked.

" O' course I zeed her."

" No," he said, " you could niver zee her zame as I do."

It was father's habit when supper was over to sit by himself in the porch and smoke, but mother would take out her knitting and draw up before the kitchen fire, the lad stretching out at her feet. He had a taste for being mothered, a thing I could never abide. None o' us talked over much, and one night I had laid my arms flat on the table and all but falled asleep 'pon top 'em, the lad turned his face up to my mother.

" Mother," he said.

" Well ? " her answered, soft-like.

" Zack's asleep—iddn't he ? "

" Ay—I reckon he be."

" Do 'ee love me, mother ? " he asked.

I kind o' smiled to myself, 'twas like the lad to be asking such—and I reckon mother thought the same, for she jest runned her fingers through his hair and didn't answer he at all.

" Mother," he said again.

" Well ? " her answered.

" 'Twas but a poor thing I made o' it."

" Us can't all succeed first-away," her answered.

" I know what 'tis I'm after having, but when I try to get it, I'm all abroad," he said, sort o' helpless.

" You be one o' the quality—and you want to take your place as such."

He drew his breath sharp in between his teeth. "I be but a poor-witted lad, mother."

"Wits iddn't everything."

"They wud help me wi' a deal I can't fathom now."

I reckon that my mother knowed well enough that the lad wasn't over and above bright, and it kind o' made her sore, though her wouldn't own to such, for her said, impatient-like, "You've got the blood anyways, there's no denying thic."

He was silent a long while after that. "It don't bring me no nearer her," he said—more as if he was speaking to hisself.

Mother knitted on, her needles clacking, now fast, now slow, and I dropped off to sleep to the sound o' 'em.

Not so very long after that the lad left us a second time. He slipped away quietful, not so much as bidding good-bye to mother, 'twas much as if he was ashamed o' going. There wasn't a deal o' money in the house at the time, still, father would ha' spared o' it, but the lad didn't ask, liking better to go empty-handed.

When it came round to the ears o' the village that the lad was off once more, they were terrible curious to learn where he had been first-along, and whether he had gone back to the same place again. Mother let fall, casual-like, that the lad had business up to Exeter, and they thought a deal o' that, till wan o' 'em happened to ask father what for a business it was, and he answered, quite unfardidle-ish—hod-boy to a mason. Hivers! but wasn't mother put out when she heard what father had done, and he was so upset at having vexed her, that the very next time her was away at Bideford market he took her kitchen range to bits and put in a special fancy-work o' his own, which drove mother more crazed than ever, because, though the oven baked well enough afore 'twas meddled with, naught would rise in it afterwards, so that she was forced to beg fa-

ther to put things back as they were, but he
said that was jest the one thing 'twasn't possible to do. Well, what wi' that and what
wi' the lad going off as he had, and us hearing naught o' un, week in week out, mother
fell ill and took to her bed. 'Twas the first
time I had ever known her do the like, and
the house got marvellous contrary, becase father, after looking wonderful consarned over
the top o' his glasses at mother, shut hisself
up wi' his work and forgot there was such
things as meal-times, much less that the time
had come for he to cook for the same.
Things soon was at a pretty pass, and
Farmer Burden told me to put the horse
into the cart and drive across and fetch Aunt
Flax from t'other side o' the hill, which I
did terrible reluctant, minding her well, having lived wi' her at the time o' the lad's illness. Her wasn't no-ways anxious to come,
and when her did, filled up the trap wi'
mops and buckets, though I told her we had
all such to home.

The first day she kept me hard at work
fetching water from the well, then her set
to and washed the house from top to bottom, not omitting father's room, but he
wasn't no-ways put out at that, because,
knowing well enough what her would be
after, he had made a contrivy-chair that
worked on wheels, a table in front o' the
same, and kept buzzing in and out o' the
house at a terrible pace, upsetting the buckets, and taking Aunt Flax herself in the rear
more than once.

" Her won't bide here long if you keep on
at that, father," I said. He stopped quat
and winked at me over his spectacles, a
thing I had never seen him do afore—then,
catching sight o' Aunt Flax, he buzzed off
on her track, and I marked by the way her
skipped up the stairs that she, for her part,
had no great fancy for his company. Howsoever, not belonging to they that be easy
bent, Aunt Flax got up that night and
burnt father's contrivy-chair, and after that

'twasn't long afore her had the house clean, neat and quiet. Once ill, mother didn't take no heed o' getting better, but lay all day, her eyes fixed on the door, as if her expected each minute 'twud open and the lad trapeze in. The news o' her ailing got to Miss Bet, and one dimmet, when Aunt Flax had dozed off afore the kitchen fire, the little lady stole up the stairs and knocked at mother's door. I reckon mother half thought 'twas the lad, for she riz up in bed and her face growed pink as a rose.

"Come in," her said, and in comed the little lady. 'Twasn't more than one look that mother gave, then she lay down and turned her face to the wall.

The tears sprang into Miss Bet's eyes. "Oh, Zack," her said, "I oughtn't to have come."

"Ay," mother repeated, "you oughtn't to have come."

I felt terrible ashamed. "Mother," I said, "'tis the little lady come to see 'ee."

At that mother sat up once more and kained into Miss Bet's face. "Bodies and souls," she tummil'd out, "but you be like one t'other."

The little lady laughed gentleful. "Do you hear that, Zack?" she said. "We are no giants, either of us."

"'Tis the lad she be thinking o'," I answered.

Miss Bet reddened a bit. I reckoned her wasn't altogether pleased to be put in mind o' the likeness. "He," she said, "where is he?"

"Ay, where be he?" my mother repeated, looking across the dimmet at the closed door beyond.

"Her's wearying for un," I said.

The little lady leaned over and took mother's hand.

"Are you wearying for him, Martha, dear?" she asked.

"Ay, I'm wearying for un."

"Poor Martha! He will come back."

"But I'm wearying for un."

Miss Bet rose and went to the windy. "He *will* come back," she repeated.

The dimmet growed darker, so that one couldn't zee the face o' t'others. I was jest about to light the candle when I heard steps sort o' feel their way up the stairs. Mother riz up in the bed, listeningful. Then the door opened once more and the lad hisself comed in.

"Mother," he said, "be you here, mother?"

She put out her hands, and a queer, choked sound struck agin the throat o' her, but her didn't say naught.

"Mother," he cried, sort o' triumphful, "I've fathomed it, though I ain't a-done it yet."

"Ay, I knowed you'd fathom it," her answered.

"I be gwaying to colonise. I be gwaying to Australie," he tummil'd out. "A man can do a deal over to there."

She clasped her arms round un. "No, no, you would niver come back to me."

"Ay, that I will, and to her."

"But 'tis far, and how will 'ee get to such an outlandish place?"

"Work my way afore the mast. Plenty o' lads ha' done it. 'Tiddn't more'n a matter o' dree months or so."

"Oh," she sobbed, "but the sea that lies atween 'ee and it."

"The sea!" he repeated contemptful. "What be the sea?"

She put a hand over his lips. "Don't speak lightzome o' the sea, lad, or maybe 'twill be after having 'ee."

"Why be 'ee in bed?" he asked all-to-once. "'Tiddn't night."

"I be gitting old."

"Old," he repeated, kneeling down beside her. "You'll dance at my wedding."

She held his face atween her two hands. "And who be 'ee after marrying?"

At that he dropped his head sudden-like down top her knee.

"I be naught to her," he cried, kneeling kind o' dispairful.

"Come," said mother, sharp-like, "give me the shawl, lad. You must be nigh starving." And he gived it her.

"Ay, I be a bit hungered, but I will bide where I be and wait," he said.

Mother gapnested dispairful round at us in the dimmet and stole out o' the room, and the little lady rose, he castings eyes on her as she stood, half-amused, half-shamed, facing him.

"I am afraid," she said, "I have let you make me partner to all your plans."

He came closer, but did not say aught.

"And so you intend to colonise?"

"Yes."

"Why?" she asked, looking curiously at him.

"Becase, becase," he tummil'd out, "there be sommat I can't reach noways else."

"Money?"

"No, 'tiddn't money, though I'll have need o' it."

" What, then ? "

He opened and shut his hands nervous-
like. " Maybe you would only laugh if I
was to tell ? "

" No, I should not laugh."

" But you hold my speach for queer," he
said, edging nearer and kaining sort o' anxious down on her.

She half turned away. " I find nothing
the matter with it."

" 'Tiddn't like speach o' yours."

" Well, perhaps not altogether," she answered, the corners of her mouth twisting
up into a smile.

" I knowed well enough you couldn't but
laugh at me," he said, drawing back.

" But I'm not laughing. Why should I
be ? "

He looked closely at her as if to make
sure 'twas truth her was speaking.

" Well ? " she said. " Well ? "

And at that all-to-once the tears sprang to
his eyes.

" 'Tiddn't naught but that I want to be sort o' equal wi' the rest o' 'em."

She took his hand. "Equal to whom?" she asked, soft-like.

"To they I comed from."

"And they?"

"They was ginelfolks."

She smiled up at him, half-amused, half-sad to one.

"And will that be so great a business?" she asked.

"I reckon to fathom it," he answered, drawing himself up proudful.

"Then you must not be ashamed of being yourself."

" 'Tiddn't that I be ashamed o' what be there." He stopped quat.

"Well?"

"A terrible deal iddn't there, and I don't know where to lay hands on it."

"It is like that with all of us."

"Not wi' 'ee," he muttered, soft-like, to hisself, though I reckon the words reached her, for she turned away half-smileful.

" I thought," she said, "that you were starving."

He didn't pay no heed to thic, but kained across the fields at the church, that stood terrible apart amid the graves. The moon rose and gapnested through the window at him and at her, and I thought as I looked at 'em that they was more'n usual like one t'other. He covered his face wi' his hands. " I shall never fathom it," he cried, bitter-like. " I feel I shall never fathom it."

A wonderful deal o' pity creeped into her eyes.

" Hush ! " she said, "it is only the world that is so stupid." But I marked that when her had spoke the word her drawed herself a little apart as if her held there was quality and quality.

"Seems terrible far away all-to-once Aus-tralia," he said.

" But you will come back."

"Ess. I shall come back."

"Why," she said, smiling, "in four years I shall be of age. You must be back in time to wish me well."

And he said he would.

A deal o' dust from the quality's carriages blowed in upon our cottage after the going o' the lad, for the Hall was full o' great folk, so that even Miss Elizabeth's wing had to be thrown open, and lights shone from the windies wi' the creeping in o' dimmet. Many a time on a still night the chime o' laughter would travel down the hill us-wards, wonderful free-flowing 'twould sound, for less stands atween the quality and their laugh than atween us and sich. When the noise o' it tippy-toed in upon us, mother would stop knitting and frown, only after a bit to set to faster than ever. Us didn't talk much now o' an evening, but whiles mother would look across at me and say, " Do 'ee reckon us 'ull soon be hearing from the lad ? "

I niver made no answer, becase her knowed
as well as I did myself that he wasn't no
hand wi' the pen. Howsomever, that didn't
stand in the way o' her putting the same
question to father when he comed in from
having his pipe, and he would look over the
tops o' his spectacles at her sort o' unseeful.

"What lad be thic?" he would say.

"Why, our lad," her would answer, indig-
nant-like.

"Be he much o' a hand wi' the pen or
no? I don't rightly remember," he would
ask.

And at that mother would pick up her
knitting and clack the needles together till
the stitches fair tumbled from the steels.

"Bodies and souls, Ebenezer!" she would
burst out, "but it was a lone day for me
when I let you put the ring on my finger."

He'd kain at her a moment questionful-
like, then a dimness would creep across the
face o' un, much as if his mind was shad-
dered back from the ordinary, and he would

drop slowly into a chair, settle his glasses, and hike away in upon hisself.

They Sundays the Hall pew was full o' great folk, and seemed bigger and squarer and more imposeful than ever. Mother dearly liked the sight o' what her called " a ripple o' quality in a congregation," and made a point o' going to church mornings for the pleasure o' setting eyes on 'em. Howsomever, one Sunday Miss Bet sat all alone, save that in the carved seat over agin her was a lad that might ha' been about the age o' our own. Quality he looked all over un, and I couldn't help but lean across to mother and say, " There would be no mistaking he for what he is, dress un how you would."

Her shut her mouth tight and tended such a deal to the prayer-book in front that there was never a moment to cast a second look at un. Wi' the ending o' service he and the little lady hiked back to the Hall together, me and mother stepping just half a field behind. He moved that free and yet that proudful, I couldn't but call to mother to mark him once again.

" Never tell me," I said, " that there ain't quality and quality."

" And be you vool enough to reckon," my mother answered, angrified, " that if he had mixated with naught but such as us he would ha' been other than the lad ? "

" Ay, that I do," said I ; " you've only got to mark his face to see that."

" And what be there so out o' ordinary in the face o' un ? "

" 'Tis brainful."

" Brainful," repeated my mother, laughing sort o' uneasy and contemptuous. " Hasn't the lad a head on his shoulders ? "

" Vath yes, but 'tis the head o' a vool."

" Out on 'ee to call un such. He'll live yet to larn 'ee the need o' better manners."

" No," I answered stubbornly, " I shall feel contemptful o' un to the last."

" You dursn't say it."

" Yes, I dare. I can't abide quality that ain't quality."

" Quality," repeated my mother, disdaineous. " Your quality be all clothes and fine speech, but God Almighty would have 'em be sommat else aside that, I reckon."

" And what would He be after having 'em ? "

" Tenderful for others, for wan."

I burst out laughing. " Hivers ! I could be thic myself."

Mother waited sort o' patient till I had had my laugh out, then her dropped down beside the path.

" Be your feet hurting 'ee ? " I asked.

" No," she said, " no. I weary for the lad, thic be all."

Father, who had been walking gazeful a few paces behind, comed up at this.

" Do you know who thic was ? " he asked. " Why, none other than the Squire o' Chickenham Chase, nevy and heir o' Black Mark Hay who shot hisself."

"Lord help us!" exclaimed my mother, "and what is he doing along wi' the little lady? The squire will never have her marry a Hay."

"'Tis said he favours this un, and the estates adjoin."

"Bodies and souls!" exclaimed my mother, "and Chickenham Chase might ha' been the lad's. To think that so much hangs on the marriage lines."

"That is how it should be," father returned. "If us can't have law and order in our hearts, leastways let us have it in our punishments."

Mother slowly rose to her feet. "There's a deal o' the shouldn't in the should, Ebenezer," she answered; "and I've never known a punishment yet fall altogether on the right man's shoulders. What call is there for the lad to be punished for his parents' ill-doings?"

"You undervallies what 'tis to be alive at all;" and then, his thoughts wandering off to other things, "There's a painful lot o' waste wi' the sun," he said, thoughtful-like. "I should dearly like to ha' the handling o' un, if it wasn't for more'n a day."

"For the land's sake, don't meddle wi' thic," said mother, "for if so be you do, 'twill never go reg'lar afterwards, I can promise that."

But father was no-ways put out. "I reckon more would grow to the acre if I did," he answered.

"I would a deal liefer starve in a natural fashion."

"Like as not," continued father, paying no heed to the interruption, "I should roast half Dunstable Weir on that day—accidental."

"Bodies and souls o' us!"

"Accidental, mind, accidental," he repeated, kaining round, interested-like, on the village.

"Oh, you idle hands beloved o' Satan! Oh, you Gomorrohish man!" cried mother, now thoroughly alarmed. "Never let me find you as much as give a look at the sun, for, mark me, if I do, I'll throw all they whirry-go-nimble tools o' yours at the back o' the kitchen fire."

"I can't make no promise," he answered, importantful.

It wasn't many days after that Farmer Burden set me to hoe turnips in a field close 'longside the river. June was well on, and the swallows and swifts were switching across the water terrible satisfied wi' life. The corn stood green on the hill above, and a fine smell o' hay comed from the meadows over agin where I stood. I wasn't working pushful hard, knowing well enough that, if I lived long enough, I should have my fill o' it, but jest stopped from time to time and kained about me. I could see the little lady, seated aneath a willow, wi' three big roses pinned in among the white o' her shadeful hat. Her was 'mazing pleasant to look on, and I left the row I was hoeing and moved

to some turnips lower down. After a bit
the young Squire o' Chickenham Chase
comed sauntering along t'other side o' the
stream. " Hivers," said I to myself, " bang
me, but I might step a bit nearer and lose
naught by it."

So I moved a row or so lower down, and
by that time the young squire had caught
sight o' Miss Bet and was hurrying his
gait.

" Why was Fate so kind and yet so
cruel ? " he said, lifting his hat and neglect-
ing to put it back on his head. " She brings
me here and yet leaves me on the wrong side
of the stream."

" Jump it," replied the little lady, sparing
just one tiddleliwinkie glance to him from
under the brim of her hat.

" But would you think the better of me if
I fell in ? "

" It would not change my opinion of you
in the least," said she, her head still bent
down over her book.

At that he kained across rather questionful. "It looks a trifle broad and deep."

"And muddy," the little lady put in.

"But Fate would not insist on my stick-
ing to the bottom, surely?" he asked, show-
ing those strong white teeth of his in a
smile.

"No, you fall in and—gurgle."

He drew back a step at that, and the
little lady returned terrible willing to her
book.

"The part does not fit me," he said.
There was silence for a while, and then he
hiked forward again and kained, marvellous
thoughtful, first across and then into the
water. "The devil!" he said.

"What did you say?" she asked, interested-like.

"No fellow could jump it."

"I've seen it done."

"Well, I don't envy him his sousing."

"Apparently not."

He was silent a long time after thic, but

at last he sat hisself down determineful as near the edge of the water as it was possible to get.

"Betty," he said.

There wasn't no answer.

"What book is that you are reading?"

There wasn't no answer.

"Why do you look so cruelly pretty?"

"What's that you say?" she asked, tilting up her face.

He jumped to his feet. "Oh, damn the stream," he said.

"Is that all?" she answered, and went back once more to her book, and he had naught left to do but sit hisself down a second time, which he did rueful enough.

"Betty," he began again.

There wasn't no answer.

"I adore you."

"What's that you say?" she asked, sparing him just one glance more.

He dug his heel, angrified, into the ground. "I love you!" he cried, fierce-like.

"Oh, is that all?" she answered, and turned a leaf of her book.

He picked three big black-headed soldiers and chopped off their nobs one after t'other, the doing o' which seemed to put him more at one wi' hisself, and he began all over again from the beginning.

"Betty!"

No answer.

"Betty!"

"Well?"

> "'Two little feet crept in and out,
> Like mice, beneath her petticoat,'"

he said, kind o' talking to hisself.

She shifted her eyes from her book to they two tiddleliwinkie feet o' hers, and then drawed 'em, terrible regretful out o' sight.

"Oh, Betty!" he cried, dismayed-like.

"Well?"

"How could you be so cruel?"

She kained up at the big sheet o' blue overhead. "Was that a drop of rain?"

"Oh, Betty," sort o' alarmed and reproachful to one. 'Mazing slow and resolved the little lady rose to her feet, and hiked wi' terrible small steps away.

" Betty ! " he cried. " Betty—oh, Betty ! "

That week Aunt Flax left us, and father was so content to see her go that he made a 'mazing contrivy lamp-wick out o' some stuff the squire gave him called asbestos, and which, set a-soak and alight, would burn untrimmed till the Day o' Judgment. Hivers! but Aunt Flax thought a deal o' father after that, though there wasn't no lamp in Dunstable Weir or they parts that the wick would fit, and she was forced to stand it in a saucer o' oil in her parlour windy, where it made a fine show o' burning on Sunday and market nights.

A matter o' three months went by before us heard aught o' the lad, and then the postman brought mother a packet wi' a tiddleliwinkie pair o' wings inside, the like o' which had never been seen in Dunstable Weir before. The letter told us how they was the

wings o' a fish, though no one outside o'
mother put faith in the tale, and powerful
pleased she was to be made acquainted wi'
the like, reckoning that the lad must ha'
reached successful parts if fish flew there.
After that her passed through a deal o' waiting afore the lad gave thought to her again,
which he did by sending her a whip wi' a
lash fourteen feet long and a bullock's tail
drawed over a stick by way o' a handle.
'Twas the most high-fangular whip the village had ever set eyes on, and there wasn't
a man in the parish who didn't ask for the
loan o' a crack wi' it, though the most didn't
do more than hang theirselves on the lash;
still, one lad there was who knowed an unusual lot o' the nature o' whips, and he drew
a sound out o' it like the busting o' cannon,
after which he hiked straight away home,
packed his bundle, and set out for foreign
parts that night, and everybody agreed that,
cracked at a wedding, church bells wouldn't
touch it for sound or style.   Miss Bet heard

tell so much o' the whip that she came down
from the Hall on purpose to see the same,
but mother put on a chariness and said that it
was put away in peppered paper for fear o' the
moths, and it wasn't till the little lady had
begged most particular that she was allowed
to set eyes on the whip at all. Howsoever,
when at last mother did bring it down,
and stretched the lash out full length along
the floor, Miss Bet stared down on the
same 'mazing intent, though I have my
doubts if her was seeing further than her
thoughts.

"Who is he, Martha?" she asked all-to-
once, and mother was so took aback that
she picked up the whip and brought down
a china dog and a text wi' the lash.

"Bodies and souls o' us!" she exclaimed,
"but this whip was never made for company."

"Well, and who is he?" repeated the little lady.

"The lad?" said my mother, in a question-

ful voice, though she knew well enough that
'twas he Miss Bet meant.

"Yes."

"Oh," mother answered, kind o' unconsarned, "just a lad wi' blood in un."

The little lady stooped down and picked
up the lash o' the whip, turning it over
thoughtful-like in her hand. "But whose
blood?" she asked.

I reckon, had mother dared, she would
dearly o' liked to ha' spoken out. "Let his
face speak for un," she said at last.

Miss Bet raised her head, and, catching
sight o' her own face in a small glass over
agin where she sat, the blood flared up to
the brow o' her, and mother, half-flusticated,
stood gapnesting down on the little china
dog that was lying all to bits upon the floor.

"Well," exclaimed the little lady, jumping
up and shaking her skirts as if the room and
us had become mighty distasteful all-to-
once, "I must be going. But that is a beau-
tiful whip o' yours, Martha," she added, her

eyes falling on my mother, who stood de-
jected-like, "and I am sure there will never
be such another in Dunstable Weir." Then,
nodding to us both, away she tripped before the red had scarce time to die out o'
her face.

It was just about then a letter came from
the lad, and, though mother was mortal
pleased to get the same, it laid a bit heavy
on her heart, because 'twasn't no-ways hard
to see that things weren't prospering wi' un.
The "Back Blocks," as he called the place,
and, wherever 'twas, they hadn't seen rain
for eighteen months. Father was terrible
interested in the hearing o' that, reckoning
that ways should be used wi' such weather.
It seems that work wasn't easier to get over
to there than here, and the lad had done a
deal o' tramping. Howsomever, he said,
'less a man got lost in the bush, which from
his account was wide-spreading and wayless,
he hadn't no need to starve, because he could
always be sure o' getting a pannikin o' flour

and a pinch o' tea from the squatters, they
being the squires out to Australia, only the
following morning he must walk on, 'twas
the walking on that came so cruel hard after
a bit.   He said that, if it hadn't been for the
drought, he reckoned he would have fathomed things better, but he hadn't no fear
but that he would get to the bottom o' 'em
at last.   As for the rest, he said he was glad
to have come, because the world was a wonderful place, whether a man prospered or
wasn't doing more than jest getting along.
Mother was no-ways to be down-hearted, and
he sent her a pair o' green-hide hobbles
which he had made himself out o' the skin
o' a bullock that had died o' thirst.   Dunstable Weir had seen hobbles afore, but they
all called round to ha' a look at these, and
Farmer Burden went so far as to ask for the
loan o' 'em for an over-wilely bay mare o'
his.   The moment the critter felt 'em on her
legs her gave such a bound that the thong
bust, and the village never thought so high

o' Australia afterwards. Still, that didn't
prevent folks from being more than usual
interested in the letter itself, and Slippy-
tongued Will, who keeps the Red Lion, of-
fered father free beer for one night just to
sit in the bar o' the inn and read the same
every time the church clock telled the half
hour. Howsomever, when father got there
he found he had left the letter at home, but
having a loose feel in his tongue, he set to
and telled them a deal o' what Australia,
would be like if he had the handling o' it,
and everyone said that, from all accounts
'twas a backward place, and they were glad
for their part that they had bided in Dunstable Weir.

After a bit, news o' the letter got to the
little lady's ears, and a message came down
from the Hall that she would like to cast
eyes on it, but mother, though her had read
the same proudful enough to the village,
kind o' held away from the letter being laid
afore the great folk. When I said that such

high-puff-dum was hard to fathom, she answered that the lad was as much quality as the little lady, and it was for he her was acting in the matter. Howsomever, the following week Miss Bet brought her watch down for father to clean. The church clock had struck the half after six, and I had just left work and was coming through our gate when I caught sight o' her standing at the door. Father was at work behind the little bench inside the shop, and was so terribly interested in what he was handling that he never marked who was there. His spectacles were perched high up on his forehead and they brown eyes o' his fixated on the skiddick between his fingers.

" What have you got there, Eben ? " asked the little lady, who had been watching him amused-like. Everyone outside my mother called father Eben.

Father looked up and smiled. He and Miss Bet had been terrible friendsome ever since the day when, as a tiddleliwinkie snip o' a child, her had brought him three fish hooks and a ball o' string to make a trap for the Hall governess.

"A little contrivy o' my own that works on a wheel," he answered, holding it up to the light.

" Why," she said, " it looks like a spoon."

"The same," he answered, " and self-acting."

" How valuable for jam ! " she exclaimed.

My father looked sort o' satisfied first at the spoon and then up at the little lady's face. " There isn't a man in the parish, or *out*, that ever hit upon its like afore. Once set going, 'twill stir till the works run down."

" Dear me ! " said the little lady, picking up the spoon and carrying it to the window. " You got a letter from Australia the other day. Didn't you, Eben ? " she asked, casual-like.

" I believe us did," father answered, not special interested.

" And how is he getting on ? "

Father was silent a bit, and then all-to-once he kained up terrible bright-eyed. " I should dearly like to ha' the handling o' Australia," he tummil'd out, " if 'twasn't for more than a week."

" Why ? Isn't he prospering there ? "

" For eighteen calendar months not a drop o' rain has fallen over to there," said my father, gapnesting sort o' blind-eyed in front o' him. " Rain should be *made* to fall there."

" Of course it should," agreed the little lady. " Let me see the letter, Eben."

" There be a power o' ways rain could be made to fall."

She looked at him, vexed and amused to one. " You forget I am only a woman and can't understand such things," she said.

" So you be," he answered, pittyful-like. " I took the letter down to the Red Lion to read to 'em," he said, searching in his pockets, " but when I got there I reckoned to ha'

left it at home; howsomever, 'twas safe in
the tail o' my coat all the time. And here
it be now," he ended, drawing the letter out.

She carried the letter over to the windy
and read it through three times, first quick,
then slower, then mortal slow. I marked
that because I watched her, wonderful surprised.

"Well," said father, "'tis but middling
he's doing, I fancy, Miss Bet."

"I'm afraid so."

The room was silent a while, and father
picked up the spoon and began to set it.
"He took a deal o' hope away wi' un."

"I wish," cried the little lady, "that he
hadn't."

"A man's never more alive than when
he's hoping, Miss Bet," father answered, sort
o' smileful.

She came closer and looked into father's
face. "Tell me, Eben, does he belong to
those who had better not have been born?"

His face growed dreamful-like under the

little lady's eyes.   "Be there such?" he
asked half o' her and half o' hisself.

"Yes, Eben, yes."

"I ha' my doubts o' it, Miss Bet."

"He can never be what he wants.   And
what can he be?"

"Thic that he was made for."

"Oh," she said, "I would like him to succeed in being what he wished—or never to
have wished."

Father took off and wiped his spectacles
terrible careful afore resettling 'em on his
nose.

"I reckon," he said, "that the lad be sort
o' dreamin' jest now."

"That's it.   He's dreaming, Eben.   And
we have all been content to let him
dream."

"'Tis through our dreams us be made,
Miss Bet."

She frowned and bit her lip.   "That's
no comfort.   Why does he dream such
stupid dreams?"

"Thic be the nature o' 'em. They be always a bit beyond us."

"Well, I don't dream," said the little lady, decisionful. "Do you, Eben?"

"I've had 'em wi' the rest, Miss Bet."

"What was your dream, Eben?"

His eyes fixated theirselves on sommat terrible far away. "To have the handling, if 'twas only for an hour, o' the big—the same, maybe, as fire, or water, or air."

"Oh!" cried the little lady, considerable took aback. "What would you do with such things?"

Father rose from his chair and sort o' growed wi' the press o' the longful wi'in un. "I should make they bigger by the whole size o' me, and me bigger by the whole size o' they," he answered.

I reckon the talk had got a bit too flambusticum for Miss Bet. She looked at father, kind o' measuring he and his dream, the one agin t'other, and then, woman-like, her thoughts tripped off elsewhere.

"Eben," she said, "I will tell you a secret Can you keep it?"

"I will do my best."

"Well, then, I'm engaged to be married."

"Now, that I hadn't thought on."

"Yes," she repeated, sort o' seriousful, "I'm engaged."

"And who to, Miss Bet, if I might ask?"

"Mark Hay."

"What, young Mark o' Chickenham?"

"Yes."

"Ah!"

"Well, Eben?"

"Naught, Miss Bet," father answered, taking off his spectacles and rubbing them against the sleeve of his coat.

The little lady's lower lip thrust itself atwart her teeth. "What are you thinking of, Eben?" she demanded, masterful-like.

"You'll make a handsome couple. There was never one o' your family, or his either, that failed in looks."

" That was not what you were thinking of."

" 'Tis true for all o' thic."

She came closer. " Eben, how can you ? " she said, codoodling-like. " When you and I are such friends, and I stole all those evil-smelling powders just for you to blow yourself up with."

" So you did, Miss Bet, so you did," father answered, softening.

" Well ? "

" I was jest reckoning back on t'other lad."

She fell silent at that, the colour flared across her face. Her always seemed a bit ashamed o' un when he was mentioned sudden-like. " I hope he will get on," she said, sort o' kind o' contemptful to one, and, nodding to father, she tripped away out o' the shop.

Not a power o' weeks after that, mother got her last letter from the lad. Length wasn't in it, three lines covering the contents. Gold, he said, had been found near where he was, and there wasn't no reason why he

shouldn't find the like hisself. I hadn't but
jest come in from work when mother told
me to change my clothes and take the letter
up to the Hall right away. The little lady
was gathering roses in Miss Elizabeth's garden. Dew was jest on the fall and the air
amazing sweet wi' the scent o' things, so
that I wondered if 'twas the earth, the roses,
or the banging great slabs o' green grass
that carried the biggest nosegay. Miss Bet
stood over against a rose-bed that was
shaped heart-fashion. Her dress was white
and shadowful in the dimmet. At sight o'
me there she laid her scissors back in the
basket and held out her hand for the letter.
She read and folded and made as if she was
about to give it back. Then the fancy took
her to read it once again.

"I wonder," she said, more to herself
than me, "if he finds gold, whether that will
help him ? "

It seemed such a foolish question, even
from a maid, that I didn't feel called to

make answer, and the little lady, picking up the scissors, cut the stems o' three 'mazing black red roses. I never was no hasty admirer o' women folk, but I couldn't but cast an eye on the little lady standing among the flowers and looking wonderful much one o' 'em herself. All-to-once she raised her head and kained up at the long row o' black windies gapnesting, sort o' sightless fashion, above her.

"Zack," she said, "why was it always in *this* garden, before these windies, that he played?"

"Hivers!" thought I, "shall I be after telling?"—and I reckoned I would, telling being pleasant work. Still, I was a bit afear'd—because I knew well enough that neither father nor mother nor the lad hisself would have had me bide silent.

"This be Miss Elizabeth's garden," I said.

"Yes."

"And they were Miss Elizabeth's rooms."

"Well?"

I stooped and picked up my cap, that had fallen from my fingers. " Thic was the reason," I answered. The flowers must have slipped from the little lady's hand, because when I raised my head the roses lay all o' a heap, the basket a-tilt beside them, and the little lady was walking, slow-paced, away.

" 'Twasn't much o' a tell, after all," said I to myself. " I reckoned to ha' drawn it out more."

With the breaking up o' the year mother grew suddenful old, putting all her tight-waisted boots away in paper on the top shelf o' the kitchen cupboard and wearing her old felt slippers, honest-like, day in and day out. Sundays, me and father hiked to church by ourselves, though mother never forgot to ask what quality had sat in the Hall pew and the name o' the text that had been preached over them.

" I likes to think o' 'em sitting there sort o' above texteses," she would say, and father would smile first at her and then to hisself.

"Parson Jack was powerful plain on sin for all o' that," he'd answer.

"Sin!" mother 'ud repeat, contemptful-like; "'tis a queer, but I never was no over-bold believer in sich."

At that father wud wipe his spectacles against the sleeve o' his coat and nod across the room at me.

"Unwisdom, then," he wud say, sort o' questioning.

"Ay, us all fails o' wisdom," mother wud answer.

Dunstable Weir spent a deal o' spare time wondering if the lad would light on gold. Most o' 'em reckoned that he would, because another lad who belonged to Dore Apple, the next village but one, had come back along home from foreign parts wi' no less than five hundred pounds sewn into his leather belt. 'Twas all in sovereigns, and he wore 'em next to his skin, and painful mar-kated he was from the same. When the months kept threading themselves one 'pon

top t'other and nary a mention o' luck, good
or bad, came, the village held that 'twas
either a fortune or nothing the earth had
given up to him. Howsomever, Dore Apple
took upon itself to be contemptful, and at
that more than one person in Dunstable Weir
said that they knowed for a fact that the lad
had found gold, though they wouldn't go so
far as to tell how they came to larn the same.
Mother listened to the clack terrible silent
for her, though I marked that her fingers
went twitterty-snip, just for all the world
after the fashion o' her tongue in days gone
by. I reckon myself that her was in thic terrible need o' success for him that she dursn't
make mention o' the word.

It was on the night afore the little lady
came o' age that he stepped in upon us once
more. The hammer o' the church clock had
riz wi' a creak afore banging out the first
stroke o' twelve, and Dunstable Weir, who
had been all hands and feet since sunrise,
was stretched out fast asleep. Mother had

been restless all day, and us had been forced to move her bed so that she could see the road that wound from the village past the three wind-twisted firs to the Hall. I had been asleep an hour or more when she came and shook me by the arm.

"Zack," her said, "do 'ee hear aught?"

"No," I answered, none too pleased. "What should I hear?"

"I'm deaf and old, and yet I sort o' hear un," she said.

"If 'tis the lad you mean, you had best get back to bed, mother, for certain sure he'll no return to-night."

Her drawed nigh the windy. "I can't see the same as I did once," her said, "and yet I sort o' see un."

I kained out across her shoulder. The moon was up and the earth shadder-stained, but there wasn't no signs o' he.

"There's naught on the road lest 'tis the shadders," I answered.

"My heart sees un, my heart hears un."

"Git back to bed, mother; you'll be taking cold."

"I shall take no cold to-night."

At that he trod out o' the dimmet, up the road and through the gate.

"Mother," I said, a bit hushed, "you see un now?"

"No," her answered, pressing her face up agin the windy-pane, "I can't see un."

"But you hear the steps o' un, surely?" I said, for they rang terribly loud on the stillfulness o' night.

"No," she answered, agape wi' listening, "I hear no steps o' un."

"But, mother," I said, "he's at the door."

"The latch be up."

"He's on the stair."

She turned and tottered and held out her hands. It didn't take more than one glance at the lad to see that 'twasn't gold he'd found.

"Mother," he said. "Mother!"

Seeing them standing there, the thought

came over me that there were big things in
the world beside gold, and then I minded
what a terrible big thing gold was.   Let
that be as it may, certain enough he hadn't
found it, and when, a bit later, he allowed
that he had naught but the clothes he stood
up in, and they were that poor that 'twas
only hisself that held them together, I
turned to him and said,—

"You have gone away quiet and unbeknown before, and there be time between
this and daylight to do the like again."

He looked at me surprised-like.   "Why,
don't her come o' age to-morrow?   Do you
think I've forgot that?   I reckon not."

"You bain't thinking o' going in they
clothes?"

"The very same, unless, maybe, you can
lend me a fit out."

I held the speech for unfriendsome, because he had a foot to the good o' me in
height.   "So you will put Dunstable Weir
to shame afore three villages," I burst out.

"What's Dunstable Weir to me?" he asked.

"Us be summat, I hope."

He turned to mother and took her hand. "You'll put on your best bonnet and let me walk aside 'ee—aye, mother?" he asked.

And she said she would, though clothes were a deal to her.

Howsomever, I woke him at cockleert the next morning. "If go you must," I said, "you'd best go now. Creep up, contrivy and hide behind a tree, and if so be the Lord stands your friend, no one will clap eyes on 'ee."

He gapnested me full in the face for three minutes or more. "Devil take 'ee!" he tummil'd out, and lay down once again in bed.

My clothes were new bought into Barnstaple and o' the colour o' claret. I should ha' taken a deal o' pleasure in the wearing o' 'em if it hadn't been for the sight o' he walking up the hill as bold as brass.

"He shouldn't be let do it," I said.

"Let do what?" father asked.

"Why, you don't mean to tell me you haven't marked they clothes o' his?"

"They seem sort o' usual."

"A blind man would beat 'ee at seeing," I burst out.

When Dunstable Weir clapped eyes on the lad, wi' pauper written as plain as print upon his back, they made believe not to ha' marked who 'twas; but law, that didn't help us, for the moment Dore Apple spotted him, they raised up such a howl that I would have given my new claret-coloured suit to have been at home.

"What's all the to-do about?" he asked, looking round.

"'Tis at you they be bawling, you Merry Andrew," I answered.

His face gave way a bit in colour. "Let 'em bawl," he said, stiff-like.

The Hall gates stood open and all the folks trooped in, spreading out fan-fashion. Mother and the lad turned into one of the side paths and I walked, sort o' unconnected, behind. A fine power o' quality stood on the lawns and swept to and fro under the trees, and glad enough I was to remember the seven foot o' park rails that stood atween them and the Merry Andrew. He stepped along casual-like, just for all the world as if he was dressed the same, or better, than other folk. I couldn't take my eyes off him, reckoning to see him seek shelter behind each tree we came to, but he passed them by as if he had never known what 'twas to hide in his life. Just to one side o' the last pair o' gates was a banging great stone, most nigh as big as our cottage.

It was hollowed out circle-fashion, and in the middle o' it grew an alder tree. Mother, who had been forced to halt a score o' times on the way, said she would like to rest a while, so we sat ourselves down under the shade of the stone. All-to-once the lad, who had been kaining about him considerable, clapped eyes on the little lady, and at that up he hopped up and away he went over the grass and through the big gates, for all the world as if the place belonged to him.

"Great God Almighty!" I said to mother, "if he bain't quality, he has the cheek o' such," and I made haste to get as close to the rails as I dared, to see what would befall, and mother, half crying wi' fear and pride, crept up beside me. The great folks, reckoning, no doubt, that the ragged gawkin was either mad or drunk, stepped back instinctive, leaving the little lady standing alone.

When she marked who 'twas coming so boldacious, she went a few steps to meet him and kained proud-like into his face, which had naught in it but the need o' seeing her, and 'twas easy telling that neither o' they two gave thought to who craned forward, curious as village folk, to see their eyes-ful.

"I minded the day," he said.

"And the gold?" she asked.

"I never struck on that."

"Ah," she answered, sort o' slow.

"But I minded the day," he said again. "I minded it every hour I was awake."

The blood sort o' swept out o' her face, but she didn't answer a word, and young Squire Mark came forward and laid his hand upon her arm. First into his face and then into hers the lad kained questionful, then he turned and walked back the way he came.

Mother met him at the gate.

"Be you rested now?" he asked.

And she answered that she was.

"Then let us go home," he said.

I followed, because I reckoned that if I saw the lad safe in the house I could go back and enjoy myself wi' an easy mind. He walked along terrible silent till he came to the three wind-twisted firs, then he stopped quat.

"Who was he that dared to lay hands on her?" he asked.

"Why, young Squire Hay o' Chickenham," I answered. "Isn't he promised to her?"

"Promised to her," he repeated.

"They'll be man and wife come next Martimas."

"Man and wife?"

"O' course."

He turned and gripped mother's hands. "'Tiddn't true," he cried, protestful.

"Oh, lad, what would you have?" her answered.

He let her hands fall sort o' helpless. "I hadn't thought o' such, I hadn't reckoned on such," he said.

That was the last time mother ever left the house till she was carried out, feet foremost, atween oak boards. Not that she gave sign o' serious ailing first along. Indeed, it wasn't till after Farmer Burden took the lad on as carter, his man having got drunk at Barnstaple Fair and broke his leg, that mother regular fell together. Her didn't touch bite nor sup that day, and when the lad came home from work, father told him to make a drop o' tea and bring it up to her, but she wouldn't so much as look at it.

"Tell me summat, summat o' the things you've seen," she asked.

"There be the bush out to Australia," he said.

"Ay, what o' thic?"

"'Tis lonesomer than a man's own heart," he answered.

"Be your heart lonesome, lad?"

"Whiles, mother, 'tis."

"Ah," she said, "I've looked on life till I was tired, and I could forgive it if it wasn't for 'ee."

"'Tis a pleasant thing life," he answered, kind o' to hisself. "Many's the time I've thought thic over to Australia, riding across they plains wi' the wind o' half the world a-thrust upon my lungs."

"Ay, lad, but that isn't life."

"'Tis a deal o' it, mother."

"I'll no deny that."

He knelt down aside her. "Mother," he said, "do 'ee love me?"

"Ay, lad."

"It be a deal to me. Be it aught to you, mother?"

"Ay, lad, a deal."

"Life gived us one to t'other," he said.

It was on a Sunday she died, towards five o' the clock. Her had laid terrible peaceable most o' the day, and, though we had sat beside her, she didn't say naught, and none o' us had words. The clock in the church tower named four, and her looked up.

"I've hearkened to he these seven-and-sixty years," she said.

Father nodded across at her. "And I've wound un over forty," he put in.

The lad was kneeling aside the bed. "Have 'ee been asleep, mother?" he asked.

"Maybe I have," she answered, "for I was reckoning I was a maid again."

"A pleasant-faced maid you was, Martha," father said.

"I was thic," she allowed; "but you was an unseeing man, Ebenezer. I never held that you marked it."

"I had always eyes for you, Martha."

"Well," she said, "there was a white dress wi' a sprig o' green thrown on it that I wore in they days, and I was reckoning that I had it c _ again."

"I minds that dress well," father put in, "and the bunnit that you wore wi' it."

"'Twas the finest straw I ever had," she said.

"And the ribbon was white, wi' five narrer green stripes," he continued.

"The same," she said; "but I shouldn't ha' credited 'ee wi' the marking o' that, Ebenezer," she said, pleasedful.

"I shouldn't ha' marked it on no other woman," he answered.

Her fell silent again; then all-to-once her sat up in bed wi' a start. "I feel afraid-

like," she cried. "Gi' me hand, Ebenezer."
And father gave her his hand.

"I shall miss they contrivy ways o'
yours," she said, and wi' that she closed her
eyes and died.

We buried her under a willow in the corner o' the churchyard, and when we got
back home father went into the shop and
locked the door upon hisself. They old felt
boots o' mother's stood terrible expectant
beside her chair, and I couldn't but kain at
'em, and then there was a knock and the
little lady came in. She talked to me quiet-
like, and after a bit her asked for the lad.

I told her he was up to mother's room and
asked if I should call him down.

But she answered she wouldn't have him
worried. I said maybe 'twould be well if
her stepped up to he. Her stood undecided-
like, then her turned and went softly up the
stairs and knocked at mother's door, and, no
answer coming, her hiked in unbid. There
was a loose board atween mother's room and

mine, and, feeling curious-like, I pushed it one side and looked in. The lad was crying all to hisself terrible sore, his face pressed deep agin the pilly where mother's head used to rest, and the little lady kained down on him unmarked. When he had sobbed a while, she leaned forward and touched him, and he looked up.

His face growed still as if the sorrow had stiffened in it.

"Oh," she said, sort o' helpless, "what can one do against death?"

"'Tis just because one has such a deal that one misses," he answered.

"But that only makes it harder."

"Us can't have it both ways," he said.

She looked at him, half-pitying, half-afraid. "You won't lose courage?"

"Her wouldn't have me do thic."

"And your plans?" she asked, hesitating-like.

"Oh, they!"

"Yes."

He walked to the windy and stared past the three wind-twisted firs at the Hall, that stood so terrible prosperous big above him.

"I reckon, if I live honest it's about the size o' me."

The little lady turned away, and her face was full of the need o' helping, but she didn't say naught.

He waited till she had reached the door, then came terrible swift across to her.

"I be going away; I sha'n't niver come back." He stopped short. "But I shall always mind on the folks I knowed here," he ended, feeble-like.

Something in the words touched the speach in her. "You mustn't go like that," she burst out, passionful, "wi' no one to help, no one to care whether you succeed or fail."

"I bain't bound up in no terrible big need this time," he said.

"But you must be," she insisted. "Your need must be just as big, bigger. I used to think you had no right to big needs, but now "—she stopped quat—" I think differently."

The lad smiled to hisself like. " You and mother be most one in that," he answered. " The mother I buried to-day, the mother who tended me that mortal untiring. 'Tis her son I be, and 'tis in her footsteps I'll follow, God helping."

She kained at him 'mazing full o' thought. " I'm glad your blood and mine be the same," she said.

Then she went out and left him.

I thought 'twas a poor show of words on both sides.

THE RIGHT O' WAY

HALF-WAY atween Dunstable Weir and Dore Apple there be a small, dree-cornered field. 'Tis 'mazing green most times, becase a stream tinkles droo it, winding fust to this, then to that. Fig Tree Cottage stands at the narrowzome end o' the field, pink-faced and brown-thatched, wi' a stone-paved yard behind and wan hanging fig tree standing up in the middle o' the zame. The door o' the house be fast shut most days, but that be neither here nor there, becase folks have a right to go droo, and no one can deny 'em entrance, for the old law holds good in Dunstable Weir Parish that the passing o' a corpse makes a free way for furren feet. Still, I can't zay that any wan makes a point o' having their rightful, finding it more neighbourzome to go no further than speach in the matter, and also, maybe, they are a bit afear'd o' old Margarette Morse, who bides like a spider behind the close-shut windies. Her be a pounceful body, Margarette Morse, and it takes sich to diddle out the right o' way wance given, though, truth to tell, 'twas all along o' her that the corpse was made a present o' the zame: droo the front door and out o' the back, there lies the road, and any man can tread it, be his boots dirty or clean. A disheartzome house for the most easy-minded to live in. Single her is for love o' the corpse that laid a dead and takeful hand upo' her house, and he none other than foolish-faced Oliver—Rabbit Skins, folks called un, for selling the zame—sich is the way o' women folks. 'Twud take a far-searching eye now-a-times to zee beauty in old Margarette's brown, wrinkled vace, but in they far-a-back days her was unusual personable, and when her zot under the big fig tree, thripping her lace-bobbins in and out,

her was most as persuasive looking as a
flower. Noll Oliver thought thic, I reckon,
for each day on his rounds he wud poke
droo the broad, stone-paved yard wi'out zo
much as zaying by your leave. Last, wan
evening Matthew Morse, own brother to
Margarette, laid in wait for un wi' a marvellous pliable ash plant in his hand, and
gi'ed un a warming that wud ha' roasted the
ribs off a bullock, let alone a weasel-waisted
bag o' bones the like o' Noll Oliver. Arter
that he reckoned to ha' done wi' the lump,
but Rabbit Skins was as persistent as feeble-
couraged; and, though he never got no far-
ther than the wrong side o' the Morses' yard
gate, he was always on the contrivy how to
diddle his cowardice and Matthew Morse
to wan. Saving to my father, who was a
peaceable man and single in they days, he
didn't give tongue on the matter; Zunday
arternoons mostly he chose for the zame,
dropping in and kind o' letting his mind fall
to pieces, picking it up bit by bit again before

he hiked off home. 'Twas a quare thing, I've heard the old man say, to zee un zitting there afore the fire, they thin, trappy hands o' his hanging wistful atween his knees like a couple o' pasr e hooks on chains, till all-to-wance they wud kind o' take up the conversation theirzulves, and swingy to this and to that till 'twas giddy work keeping count o' they and the wuds togither. My father suffered terrible bad from a softening in the heel o' his right foot, and he used to be soaking the zame in hot water and half a pinch o' starch for stiffening purposes, while Rabbit Skins was loosening off his mind, and that, he zed, kind o' added a seasoning o' sense to the arternoon.

"Tobin," he wud tummil out, tarning his great, soft brown eyes 'pon my father—wonderful eyes they was, so folks zed, kind o' searching and dreamful to wan—" do 'ee know what 'tis to feel your bones ragged wi'in 'ee, much as if a puff of wind wud scatter 'em?"

" Can't zay as I do," answered the old man, though 'twas young he was in they days.

" 'Tis the will to fight I have."

" Then there's naught to prevent 'ee indulging the zame."

At that, Noll's fingers wud pick up the thread o' talk and twisty-twisty till my father got flusticated and popped his feet into the boiling water by mistake.

" Dom it ! " he'd zay.

" Ay, cuss it ! " Rabbit Skins wud chime in, " 'tis the will to fight I have, but not the power."

" Law bless 'ee," my father wud answer, his heel having cooled down a bit, " what be there in a fight, save broken bones, that you shud be so arter the giving or the taking o' 'em ? "

Noll Oliver wud rise from his chair and give the old man no peace till he hobbled across to the windy, from where wan cud git a glimpse o' the top of the girt fig tree in Morse's yard.

"Every dimmet, fair or foul, these five years I've poked by that tree while her growed from child to maid," he'd zay.

"Well, well," my father 'ud answer, "'tis the way o' young folks fust to grow up and then to grow old."

But Rabbit Skins niver paid no heed to he. "'Tis nigh on towards dimmet and I must be on the move, and, wi' that, off he wud hike, much as if he was gwaying on the zame old round o' the five past years; but, bless you, he niver got no furder than the gate afore Morse's yard, and there he'd stand and kain across at the maid, zitting terrible demure in a white mob cap, sich baing the fashion in they days. Whiles my father 'ud valler un, wishful o' larning what the two zed wan to t'other; zim'd, though, that they was most unusual zilent, zeeing that they was both young and had tongues in their heads. Howzomever, my father tells that wance the maid looked across at un proudlike.

"Why don't 'ee poke droo, Noll Oliver," her asked, " the zame as you've been wont to these five years and more ? "

At that the lad's body kind o' twitched forrard, and he put out his hands and clutched at the iron bars o' the gate, but made no move to lift the latch.

Then her axed agin, " Why don't 'ee poke droo, Noll Oliver, the zame as you've been wont these five years and more ? "

The gate zim'd to shiver, much as if 'twere alive ; but, when Margarette Morse saw that it bided shut, she rose from her seat aneath the fig tree and went back to the house, nor did she as much as tarn her eyes agin to where he stud. At the shutting o' the door ahird her, Noll Oliver pitched forrard on his vace, and Matthew Morse found un lying afore the gate, and took and flung un into the ditch on the hither side o' the road, when he fell into sich a slummock o' mud that my father felt fair ashamed o' acting the friendzome in picking un out agin.

Arter that he got more fetched in his head than iver, and many there was who thought he wud be safer inside the asylum, or least-ways the jail; but, law, he baing naught but a poor man, no wan had the time to in-terfere, zeeing well that money 'ud have to be spent on the matter. Then, wan market day when Matthew Morse was away to town, what should Noll Oliver do but take my father's old blunderbus down from the nail where it hung aside the dresser, and trapeze off wi' ut. 'Twadn't long my father was in vallering arter un, suspicioning well that he was up to no good wi' the zame; but, what wi' Rabbit Skins baing the quicker o' limb, and my father minding on the fact that the gun was loaded to busting point, the lumpkin had reached the gate o' Morse's yard jest as the old man gained the top o' the hill looking down on the zame. 'Twas a fine clear day, and my father cud zee old Margarette—though, to be sure, her was a maid in they days—sitting under the

fig tree thripping her lace-bobbins in and
out. His legs tarned to water where he
stud, for he thought for sartin sure the lad
was gwaying to do no less than shoot her.
Naught o' the kind happening, howzomiver,
my father comed down the hill at a steady
pace, always bearing in mind the fact that
his blunderbus had a way o' shooting in the
most unexpected directions. Thankful he
was that no undue hurry possessed un, for
jest as he came nigh the gate the gun went
off, whether by accident or design the
crowner or the Almighty be the best o'
jidges, but 'tis sartin that in doing so it let
fly a wonderful varrigated collection o'
slugs, nails and scraps o' old iron full in the
broad o' Noll Oliver's chest. A banging
big hole they tore out for theirzulves, and
blood, my father zed, anuff to paint a good-
sized field, welled from the zame. He and
the maid togither carried un in and stretched
un out under the fig tree, where he lay, his
brown eyes wide stretched, looking terrible

much a lad.   Margarette her knelt azide he
and took the hand o' un in hers.

"I knowed," her zed, "that you wadn't
afear'd to come."

The blood and froth was oozing from his
lips, so that he cudn't answer in wuds, but,
for a man that had jest shot hiszulf, he
zim'd wonderful plazed wi' the situation.

When Margarette Morse saw that the lad
was past speech, her rose up and shook my
father by the arm.

"Bear witness," her zed, "that he wadn't
afear'd to come."

My father he stud there scratching his
head, looking fust to wan and then to
t'other, for well he knew that either he or
they was mad.   But law, Noll Oliver died
even as her spoke, and the maid, zeeing for
herzulf that he was past recall, put her two
hands under un and beckoned to my father
to do the likewise.

"Carry un droo the house," her zed.   "In
droo the front and out droo the back, and

the passing o' his corpse shall make a free way for furren feet to tread."

My father did as her bade un, and that be the long and the short o' how there comed to be a right o' way droo Fig Tree Cottage —though folks say 'tis all o' a piece wi' Margarette Morse just to give and then to make the gift o' no account.

VILLAGE PUMP FEWINS

KITTY FEWINS'S husband wadn't zactly mad, though his ideas was a bit jambed, and he reckoned he was the village pump and had to be fed on eggs to be kept gwaying. Still, for a man that had a big appetite for food, and none for work, 'twas a thought-out taste, and came expensive on his family. Not that they complained, indeed they had all in their time been proud to work for their father, holding there wadn't his like for style o' behaviour inside the parish or out. Howzomever, saving o' Jane Elizabeth, t'others was packed away, dree in a row, in the far corner o' the churchyard; but afore they died they had done their fair share at earning the worth o' eggs. There was John Tummas, the eldest, and Coodoodling Mat, small and crooked-toothed, wi' a fine knowledge o' other folks' fowls—though the Fewins, taken as a family, was held for honest—a man that made a marvellous few words go a long way; they used to depend on he for winter eggs; last o' all, there was Poddy Peter, the youngest lad, the zame baing terrible anxious to do wi'out the power o' doing, though he wance picked up a druppenny bit on the road, which was claimed the zame arternoon. Kitty Fewins herzulf was a hard-working, rispactable body, detarmineful o' gieing the world full weight. I reckon, poor soul, it took all her strength to do it when her sons was alive to help her; and when they died there wasn't much left outzide her detarminefulness to fall back on. John Tummas was the first to go; and, arter he, a loose fall o' stones carried away Coodoodling Mat, and then comed the tarn o' Poddy Peter. Strange enough, 'twadn't the two eldest o' the sons that her missed most, but jest the small lad.

"He niver arned naught, Poddy Peter didn't," her wud zay, "but then he was thic willun." "Law," her wud continny, "he was as proud o' his father reckoning hiszulf the village pump as any o' 'em, and there wadn't a day he didn't count the shells o' the eggs, though, it zim's, 'twadn't to be his lot to do the more showy part."

Still, he was companionful to the last, and when Jane Elizabeth took upon herzulf at jest that moment to come home from sarvice wi' a housemaid's knee and the recurring twitch on the right side o' her face, wan would ha' thought 'twas her, not he, that was marked for death. Howzomiver, he it was, and the last thing that he axed arter was the egg-shells.

"Lay the breakfast wans there," he zed, "and they from dinner and tea over agin 'em."

He counted 'em out, a round dozen they comed to, while his father stud azide the bed wi' wan arm twitched out straight ahind un,

the zame as if 'twas the iron handle o' a
pump.

"Mother," the lad continnied, kaining up
in the face o' Kitty, "do 'ee reckon I'll live
over the day? becase as like as not father
'ull fancy his supper to-night."

"Yes," Village Pump Fewins chimed in,
"I shall fancy eggs to-night."

At that Kitty whipped ronnd on her man
pretty sharp.

"There be nigh on seven in the house,"
her zed, "if so be you *can* fancy 'em."

"Bile the lot," he answered, and Poddy
Peter sot up in bed and clapped his hands.

They was jest on to the bile when the
small lad died.

Outside o' groaning behind a black-edged
handkerchief in church the Zunday vollering
their funerals, Village Pump Fewins took
the loss o' his sons wonderful unconsarned.
'Twas evident that, from the point o' baing a pump, he reckoned never to run
dry.

"Eggs," he zed; "I don't ax for more'n eggs."

A terrible lot o' rain fell that winter and spring, and whether 'twas thic or the scarcity o' eggs, I can't tell, but Village Pump Fewins began to ail much arter the fashion o' Poddy Peter. Folks were sorry to think o' losing un, he baing more like an institootion than a man, and those that had a hen in lay wud send the eggs acrass to Kitty. Her, poor soul, couldn't fasten to the idea o' her husband dying, and always reckoned that wi' the coming o' warmer weather and the plentifying o' eggs he wud be hiszulf agin. Still, it zim'd, as the spring wore away, that the rain wud niver cease to fall; the floods was out, most o' the villagers had illness to home, and the churchyard growed greener and fuller each day. Wan evening I took over dree eggs to Fewins's cottage that my speckled hen had laid day and about. Village Pump Fewins was sitting up in bed, his right arm hanging like a terrible listless

handle ahind un.   At the sight o' the eggs
he kind o' stiffened all over.   Kitty kained
acrass at his face, and then reached down a
saucepan, though the supper things had long
since been washed and put away.

" I'll bile wan o' 'em now," her zed.
" Maybe he'll zlape the better for the taste o'
it.   He hasn't had an egg these five days or
more."

" Bile 'em all dree," her husband jerked
out—there was never no power o' resarve
about he.

At that Kitty popped 'em all into the
saucepan, though her sighed to herzulf, wondering, no doubt, where the next lot o' eggs
was to come from.

I was working as under-gardener up to the
Hall in they days.   The squire was a hard
man and close, wi' a terrible zeeing eye, so
that the place wadn't over-prized, saving, o'
course, that wages was paid reg'lar.   Wan
marning I started to work earlier than usual,
becase the weather had held up the last day

or so, and I was minded to sow a few seeds
afore the rain returned. Having to pass droo
the stable yard on my way to the gardens, I
stapped quat, for who shud I zee coming out
from the henhouse, her hands full o' eggs,
but Kitty Fewins herzulf. Us stud and
looked at won t'other, and I marked that her
face was more proudful than shamed.

" Good gore, Kitty ! " I zed, " whativer be
'ee doing wi' they eggs ? "

" I've stole 'em," her answered.

" Gosh ! " I zed, " I always held 'ee for
honest."

" I always held mezulf for honest," her
answered.

A terrible lot o' minutes went by, then I
axed,—

" Be he dying ? "

" Yes."

" And he fancies eggs the zame as iver ? "

" Yes."

" Ain't 'ee got no money to buy 'em ? "

" No."

"Lord ! " I zed, " I won't tell on 'ee."

Her smiled.

" I wud be better pleased for 'ee to tell," her answered. " There iddn't no call for 'ee not to be honest."

" No," I zed, " I won't tell. But maybe," I added, anxious-like, " you'll put 'em back where you took 'em from."

" I can't do thic," her answered.

My feet moved sort o' uneasy. " Well, leastways you'll take no more eggs arter this ? " I zed.

" I can't promise thic," her answered.

" Good gore, Kitty ! " I tumm'l'd out, " I always held 'ee for honest."

" Ay," her answered, " I always held me- zulf for honest."

" What's this talk about being honest ? " axed the squire, coming in upo' us un- awares. " And what's the meaning o' my eggs in your hands, Kitty Fewins ? " he added.

" I stole 'em, sir," her answered.

"There be only wan place for a thief, woman," he zed, "and that's the jail!"

"Ah," her breathed, sort o' slow.

"I never had pity on a dishonest person yet," he zed.

Five eggs her stole, and five weeks her got, a week's hard labour for each egg. There wadn't no one left to support Village Pump Fewins when her was gone, so he and Jane Elizabeth was taken acrass to the work'us. Law, he didn't live long as a bluegown. Skilly iddn't eggs, and when Kitty Fewins comed out o' jail, her husband was dead.

Her kind o' prided herzulf that naught but eggs cud keep un alive. Us niver had his like in Dunstable Weir again.

CROOKSIE

CROOKSIE wadn't no more than a small, hump-backed child wi' a wonderful fancy for aught that had a straight look to it. He lived 'long o' me, not that he was any child o' mine, though folks did give me credit for the fathering o' un. That's neither here nor there; Dunstable Weir has a bitter tongue and has always held me for plainer than I be. 'Tiddn't for me to tell who the lad's father was, or his mother either, for the matter o' thic, but I'll say this, there wadn't a sweeter-faced lass in all the countryside. Me and her used to go nutting as childer, and fust-along us shared the nuts ekal, but when her growed to be a maid her kept back the kernels, save, maybe, when two sich lay dranged up terrible close in a shell, then her wad give me wan, but I had to be most

181

unusual smart or her'd take it away agin
and eat it up herzulf. Crooksie was born
aside the big rocking stone on Dunstable
Heath, wi' the grey mist for sheet, blanket
and coverlet. I minds the night well. I'd
been azlape an hour or more when there
comed a banging girt knock at the door. I
pulled on my trousers and went to zee who
'twas. The moon was up, and when I
opened the door a terrible long shadder fell
acrass the kitchen. I hadn't no need to
look up at the man's face to larn who stud
afore me.

"Come along," he zed.

I didn't draw away an answer on sich
as he.

"Come," he zed agin. "Wud 'ee have
the maid die not having had speech wi'
'ee?"

At that I kind o' pitched a step forward
and stopped quat.

"So you have got a patch o' the love in
your blood still, for all her couldn't stomach

sich in 'ee?" he zed, laughing sort o' un-
mirthful.

I took my coat down from the peg.

" 'Tiddn't to waste words that either o' us
be standing here to-night," I answered.

" No," he zed ; " but the sight o' that squat
little body o' your'n kind o' stirs a laugh in
me every time I set eyes on it. 'Twadn't
impidence that failed 'ee in holding yerzulf
a fitting mate for the maid."

" I wudn't ha' brought her to ruin and left
her to die on Dunstable Heath," I tumm'l'd
out.

" Vule, who be you to judge your bet-
ters?" and wi' that he whipped round and
hiked off, I vallering.

A fine, stillified zilence lay 'pon top the
heath as us threaded our way to where the
rocking stone stud tippy-toe above his girt
shadder. The moon was sort o' playing at
baing big-sized, and there was a deal o' light
thrown round, careless-like, when one minds
how scant her is o' the zame at times. It

comed over me that there should ha' been
more continuous shadder, knowing, as I did,
that the maid lay dying.   Still, there was new
ways ahead o' her, poor soul, and maybe her
found the light more to her taste than I did.
Her was stretched out, a length or more
from the big stone, and the chile, a bit of
petticoat mopped round un, rasted agin her
arm.   I hadn't no words, but, rucking down,
made sort o' believe o' being spachful, and
her opened her eyes and kained into mine.

"Zack," her zed, "us sha'n't niver go nutting no more togither."

"There's pramise o' a good season this
year," I answered, though I thought to me-
zelf 'twas like the maid to talk o' outzide
trash jest then.   Maybe her knowed that
time was getting scarce, for all-to-wance the
tears pushed out o' her eyes and her tried,
sort o' tremorful, to riz; but 'twas more'n
her had the strength for, and her sank back
upo' the green sod, much as if 'twas her
grave and the Resurrection Trump hadn't

but jest stirred her. The child gie'd a little tittering scrit, and her drawed un closer.

" He ba a sma' and crooksie, Zack," her zed. " Sma' and crooksie."

I put out a careful hand and touched un.

" 'Tiddn't to be expected that his father 'ull iver own to a crooksie chile," her continnied.

There was more zilence than speech inside o' me.

" You must take un in and do you best by un," her zed, and wi' that her closed her eyes and died, stiff and angered becase I had no wuds.

Widdy Bartlett lived over agin my house in they days, and I carried the child across to her, reckoning that the sooner the little skiddick had women folk around un agin the better. Her unrolled un out o' the petticoat, and he lay, terrible red and crooksie, 'pon top her knee.

" Lord help us, but he's plain for a love child," her zed, looking vust at un and then across at me. "But there," her added, "beauty iddn't to be made out o' naught, more'n the rest o' things."

"Be he like to be healthy?" I axed, for it zim'd to me jest then that the chile might well die and no wan miss un.

"The misshapen be always long lived," her answered.

"Maybe that back o' un will straighten out wi' time," I zed.

"Na, na," her mumbled. "Nater iddn't gwaying to over-wark herzulf for un, you may take my word for thic."

And nater niver did, crooksie he was born and crooksie he bided, though from the vust he showed a winderful liking for aught wi' a straight look to it. What growing he did, he did zlow, save for his head, and thic kind o' squatted 'pon top his shoulder, and was broad and brainful. He vallered the maid as to the eyes—black they was, wicked and good, merry and sad, mixed in wan; for the rest, there was naught much to mark about

un, save, as I zed afore, that he was crooksie.

I bain't altogether a hard man, nor wan
to bear over and above heavy on the weak-
zome, but there was zommat in folks holding
the chile for mine, because he was crooksie,
that kind o' tarned me agin the crooksacious,
and he knawed it from the vust and held
back from me. Times there was I wud ha'
dearly liked to ha' passed over that he
wadn't straight-limbed, but he wud niver
let me forget it, zim'd most as if he was fair
glad that us cudn't be vriends, wan wi'
t'other, becase o' the zame. I was hard and
bitter in they days, and the chile drank o' it,
arterwards thic which was sweet in life was
niver sweet to he. It zim's to me now, looking back on it, that I only wance heard un
laugh, maybe I shudn't ha' done so then, if
I hadn't come on un sort o' unawares. 'Twas
a 'mazing hot day, and the sky was bare,
save for wan banging girt cloud, which had
lumbered into the west and got hooked up

for the want o' a few bagfuls o' wind.
Crooksie was lying on his back plump in the
dust, rain falling out o' nowhere in particular, big, wide-apart draps saucering the dust
all round un. He zim'd to have a deal to
tell up, but mostly to the rain.

"Iddn't 'ee jest a straight-fallie thing,"
he kept on zaying, and he clapped his hands
and laughed the most fresh-spoken laugh
I iver heard out o' a chile's lips.

I was that took back, I stud gapnesting at
un like a toad atop a stone, then, all-to-
wance, he comed to knaw that I was there,
and he looked acrass at me out o' they black
eyes o' his terrible malicious.

"Was 'ee making merry at the rain,
Crooksie?" I axed. But he picked hiszulf
up and didn't answer me a wud.

Jest inside the breast o' my coat I had
a kitten that I had found in wan o' the fields
when I was to work. 'Twas a terrible
mismanagement o' a critter, baing most as
crooksacious in the make as Crooksie hiszulf.

Afore I knowed what I was arter, I whipped
out the lil' skiddick and pitched un down
aside o' the lad.

"Maybe you'll take to thic un," I zed.
"You and he be much o' a make."

A curious look, sort o' angered and
shamed to wan, comed into his face, much
as if he was axing hiszelf if 'twas true that
he cut such a figure afore the world. Stoop-
ing down, he picked up an almighty big
stone and made as if he wud ha' killed the
poor misshapen critter, then he stapped quat
and the stone slipped from un. Maybe the
cat hadn't met over much o' the vriendzome
in life, for her zim'd most too frightened to
tarn tail, and stud kaining, piteous, vust up to
the chile's vace and then to mine. I felt 'mazing discomforted considering as how I was
the straight-limbed wan out o' the dree, and
I thought 'twud be well to take the cat back
to where I found her ; but when I put out a
hand to make a grab at her tail, the critter
pitched herself plump into Crooksie's arms.

He gie'd her shelter, taking her on wi' un into the house. From that day to the marning arter Crooksie's death, her lived 'long o' us. Her niver had no name to speak of, being mostly called *Thic un*. There was naught sociable about her, saving that her was always in sight. Knawing Crooksie's fancy ran arter the straight, I used to wonder to mezulf what he veeled for thicky cat. Whiles I reckoned he hated her, not that he was unkind to the critter, treating her with a wonderful fine rispact; but jest that his eyes was always zaying, "Be I crooksie the zame ez thic un?" Wance I heard un talk to her sort o' unbeknown.

Thic un gapnesting into the fire, paying no special heed to what was baing told up.

"You be fed reg'lar 'long o' us. Maybe food counts for zommat wi' a cat," zed Crooksie.

Thic un gied a sort o' stifled yawn.

"'Tis all naught agin baing crooksie," the lad muttered to hiszulf.

"You iddn't so wonderful out o' the way crooksacious," I tumm'l'd out.

Crooksie whipped round, vacing me, his lil' bentified body on the quiver wi' the anger that was in un; but not a word did he zay. For sociableness he wadn't a bit more forrard than the cat. Vust o' all, I didn't mind his baing do terrible zilent, reckoning that 'twas the nater o' the chile, but bit by bit I came to knaw that, though he niver had a wud to throw at me, he'd talk a deal to the things around un, if 'twadn't no more than a terrible tall blade o' grass. Arter thic I got in the way o' trying to catch un on the tell, but 'twadn't long afore he suspicioned me out. Many's the time I've axed mezulf what be there in some scant-wudded folk that wan wud so dearly like to ha' speech wi' 'em. Why should us reckon that sich a terrible deal be stacked away ahind their zilence? And it comed over me that 'twas a poor thing to worrit for the clack o' a chile's tongue, special when there niver had been no richness o' speech atween us.

At our end of the village there lived a good-for-naught poaching gawkin, Simeon Bag by name. He was tall and upstanding, and many's the time I had marked Crooksie kaining arter un trapezing down the road, and the thought wud come over me that, maybe, wi' sich as Simeon the chile 'ud not be silent-tongued. I niver had no call to ax the man inside, whiles I half brought mezulf to do so, and then zommat held me back from it. Howzomever, wan day Simeon walked in unbid. I was earthing taties. He didn't pay no heed to me, but walked straight up to where the chile lay aneath the apple tree. I didn't turn my head, but I kind o' knowed that they two was measuring one t'other's hearts, and all the while I was axing mezulf, "If he speaks will Crooksie answer un?" The minutes was each wonderful particular to get his own vally, there baing no scurry or up-and-done wi' it

among 'em, but when my ears fain ached wi'
listening to naught, I tarned to zee if eyes
cud put a meaning to the zilence, and there
was Simeon stretched out on the broad of
his back under the apple tree. It comed
over me, wi' a curious pain, that 'twadn't the
vust time they two had lay there, zide by
zide, and gapnested up droo the boughs at
the sky overhead. I velt more'n usual left
to mezulf, becase I had reckoned that the
lad railed off the world atween the crooksie
and the straight, and held that the wan cud
ha' no dealings wi' t'other. The vallering
day I went to my wark the same as usual,
but I shud have dearly liked to ha' hung
round, gentleman fashion, sort o' marking
who went in and out. Zim'd most as if
Simeon Bag was trying to steal zommat
from me. I velt distrustful o' un.

Crooksie had always been a terrible chile
for ailing. I often reckoned to mezulf, if
his dead mother see'd down from where her
was, her wud ha' had the same poor opinion

o' my handling that her had in life. Wan day
when the lad was close on his ninth year old
Doctor Budd pulled up 'longside me in the
road.

"You be gwaying to lose that little
crooked lad o' your'n," he tumm'l'd out.

I didn't make no answer, speech baing un-
needful, but I gathered my tools togither and
started for home. A terrible tall hedge ran
round my cottage, and I pulled up short and
kained droo, for I sort o' suspicioned Crooksie might ha' stretched hiszulf out aneath the
apple tree, which stands to your left as you
goes in at the door. There he was, sure
anuff, and Simeon Bag azide, the cat sated
a good dree veet away. For a young un,
Crooksie had always walked lonesome droo
the world, and it zim'd wonderful poor to
grudge un to the wan pursen who had tooked
his fancy, but all-to-wance my life zim'd
winnowed down to jest mezulf and my
heart's desire, and aught that stud atween
me and it took on an extry vally. Times

and times I laid awake at night figuring how I cud stap Simeon Bag from coming and yet make on to Crooksie that the fellow had desarted un for furren folk, but I never comed to a settled mind on the matter, baing sort o' wishful to do well by mezulf and the lad to wan. All this while Crooksie was dying o' the galloping-fade, so that I had but to mark back the days to zee how he was slipping away from me, and he niver so much as noting that I was in the world 'longzide o' un. Folks have always held me for zlow, and when the village larned that Crooksie hadn't more'n a few weeks to live, they comed in wan by wan to tell me the tale, believing that I cudn't take such in for mezulf. I didn't pay no special heed to what they was letting up, and that made 'em more repeatful than iver, but the lad listened to their talk terrible interasted. The last week Crooksie was wi' me, Simeon Bag was in and out continuous. It zim'd pushful o' un. I thought to mezulf that the man

might ha' had more sense, becase everywan
knaws that, wi' death in the house, there is
often a deal to be zed, and wan arternoon I
stapped un just as he had put his foot atop
the garden step.

" Do 'ee reckon to be the only pursen who
has need o' a tell wi' the lad ? " I axed.

He reddened up smart.

" Why, you and Crooksie niver ha' naught
to zay wan to t'other," he answered.

I velt curious angered, considering that
there was a deal o' truth in what he zed, but
I wasn't gwaying to argify. The vallering
day he niver comed nigh the house. I
knowed that becase I didn't go to work, but
jest bided at home to ha' a tell wi' Crooksie.
We had been unspeechful sich a terrible
number o' years, and I knawed from the veel
o' my own heart that there was a deal to zay
and only a sma' snip o' time to zay it in, but
for all thic, us was zilent the zame as iver.
I thought back on the days us had been
together, and, though I cud mind many a

sharp word I had drawed at un, yit he had niver wanted for naught, and it zim'd as how he might ha' a smile for me jest at the last. The arternoon wore on. Crooksie lay wi' his eyes fixed on the door, watching and kaining, kaining and watching. I got sort o' desperate, for how was I to know whether Simeon Bag wudn't take up hiszulf to distarb us at any moment.

I went up to the bed and touched the lad. "Zay zommat, Crooksie," I said.

He drew away much as if he hadn't heard, so I tippy-toed back to the fire, and zat there kind o' guilty, for it comed over me that I was axing the chile for a bit o' love, and all the time I was holding back from un the. wan pursen he hungered arter zeeing. Still, wadn't he as good as a son o' mine, and who shud he want to ha' wi' un at the last if it 'twadn't me?

Night was long in coming, for summer was full on, but when the room was most nigh dimmet, I stole up to un agin.

" Zay zommat, Crooksie," I zed.

Then he riz right up straight in the bed and cried out as wan zore wounded,—

" Why do 'ee bide away ? "

I went out and fetched Simeon Bag, and he took Crooksie up in his arms, and the lad stretched hiszulf out, tiredful, and died.

They niver zed naught wan to t'other. I cud swear they niver said naught wan to t'other, leastways not in words.

MARY AMELIA SPOT

MARY AMELIA SPOT belonged by rights to Dore Apple, a fishing village about a mile and a half from Dunstable Weir. 'Twadn't much o' a place, though they tell that in the time o' the Armady deeds were done off it. Nowadays, howsomever, the men were mostly a parcel o' dirty-mouthed drunkards and the women-folk hard o' tongue. Taken as a whole, there was more drangs than streets in Dore Apple, and right at bottom o' the most narrowzome drang lived Mary Amelia Spot. A plain-featured woman Mary Amelia was, and had niver, I reckon, tasted much o' the soft side o' a man's tongue till Job Tremmy comed a-courting her. Folks said 'twas all o' a piece wi' the rest o' un to hike down to

Dore Apple in search o' a wife, zeeing that 'twud be hard to meet wi' his ekal for drink up to Dunstable Weir.   Not that he didn't have his sober times, when he earned a good wage, but beer had sich encouraging ways for Job, that wance on the tap's scent there was no parting 'em wan from t'other till he had taste o' the barrel.   In drink 'twas marvellous what kindly things Job had to say about women-folk, though he saw 'em much as the rest o' us when sober.   Still, if you minded him o' what he'd said, he wudn't go back on his word, and I can most believe that that's how 'twas he and Mary Amelia Spot comed to be man and wife.   No wan iver heard tell 'zackly what happened when he clapped eyes on her fust, but wan Sunday morning he comed acrass to my cottage wi' a terrible serious face on un.

"Zack," says he, "I be gwaying a-courting, and I want 'ee to lend me a hand wi' the wuds."

I reached my hat down from the nail be-

hind the door and vallered un out. Us
didn't zay naught, and Job, he hurried along
thic fast I thought he must be wonderful set
on zeeing the maid. When us comed to the
tap o' the hill above Dore Apple he stapped
quat and rubbed the sweat off his face wi'
the back o' his hand.

"Whativer will her be like by light o'
sober sense?" he zaid to hiszulf, kind o' zarrerful.

I didn't make no answer, not having zeen
the maid, and Job, he pushed on ahead
wance again, till, after a bit, us comed to
Mary Amelia's cottage. The door stood
open, and us went in. Her was sitting, a
bucket atween her knees, peeling taties. My
wud, but her was plain! I kind o' drawed
back, thinking maybe us had come to the
wrong house; then I slipped a glance acrass
at Job and I saw un straighten up, though
his face had a divered look, as if he sore
doubted whether he had spunk to zee un
droo wi' the job. "Crikes!" says I to my-

self, "God Almighty made women, 'tiddn't for us to complain."

Job, he took a step forrard, then he tarned to me. "Clean," he says. 'Twas her one good point, and he lighted on it wonderful straight. Hearing us speak, Mary Amelia Spot raised her eyes—wan o' 'em was blue, t'other pure white 'cept a small darkish dob high up in the left corner near the lid.

"I reckoned on 'ee coming in later to take a bit o' dinner," she said. "Maybe you'll drap in agin after church, the bell's ringing still."

Us got outside and walked kind o' trembly to the end o' the drang. Then I drapped a hand on Job's shoulder.

"Run!" I says.

"Run?" says he.

"And niver come anigh Dore Apple again as long as you live," I says.

He struck his right fist into the palm of his left hand.

" Me and Mary Amelia Spot be pramised wan to t'other," says he.

" Vorgit it," I says.

At that he drowed me such a look, and, tarning, went back to the cottage wi'out another word.

The vallering Sunday he and her was called in church, and all the lads hiked down to Dore Apple to zee what the maid was like. They comed back again marvellous quiet, for they was young and didn't know but what they'd soon be marrying their-zulves. Job, he took to drinking something fearful to behold, and the more he drank the more good points he found in Mary Amelia Spot, till wan or two o' the more inexperienced went down again to Dore Apple to take a second look at her. After thic us had a wedding. Job axed me to be best man, so I stud aside un at the altar, and as I cast an eye acrass at Mary Amelia Spot I didn't vorgit to thank the Almighty that her wadn't no bride o' mine. Wance they

was married, curiosity fell asleep, the sight
o' a plain-vaytured wife having naught un-
natural about it to most folk.

Job's cottage stood over against mine—a
banging high wall ran along each side o' the
road for a matter o' fifty yards between us
and the next house. Mary Amelia was a
great stay-at-home, and the neighbours niver
drapped in, having used up all the attention they had for her, so, outside o' me, her
saw no wan. I was in to the cottage most
days, for there was sommat about the
woman that drawed me back to look at her
again and again. The amount o' work her
wud git droo in the day was wonderful to
behold. Her took in washing, and such was
her feeling for starch that the gentry for
miles round sent in their fallals, and Mary
Amelia niver failed to give 'em satisfaction.
Zeeing that money was plentiful, and not
being a competitive man, 'twadn't long afore
Job left off gwaying to work; for what was
the use o' two wearing theirzulves to the

bone? Zometimes, though, he'd call round
and collect the bills; then us could all have
a rare spree-about, for Job was open-handed
wi' the best o' 'em. I used to wonder what
the poor woman thought o' his spending the
money her worked hard to earn; but her
kept herzulf to herzulf, and Job told up fine
tales about her vartues as the drink passed
round. Indeed, most o' us was inclined to
agree wi' un, for there had niver been so
much free beer to be had in the parish since
election day.

'Twas getting well on towards Christmas
when Mary Amelia took to her bed, and the
night after her fell sick Job came acrass to
tell me he was father o' a little maid. He
wor looking a bit anxious—as well he
might, for 'tiddn't every man that had
such an earnzome woman to work for un.
I axed who the child favoured, Job being
a very passable-looking man. He didn't
make no answer for a bit, but zot hiszulf
down afore the fire and groaned marvellous

touching. All-to-wance he lifted up his head.

" Her's the very moral o' her mother, even to the eyes," he tumm'l'd out.

I wor silent, not having aught to zay, and Job, he stretched a trembly hand acrass and laid it 'pon tap my knee.

" There be two Mary Amelias in the world now," he said, " for I shall name the maid arter her mother."

Then he rose up from his chair and went away. I heard arterwards that he was in to the Red Lion, drinking zomething fearful to behold.

Mary Amelia was slow to take strength, and one might zay that her niver rightly got back to herzulf again, though, as soon as her could move, her slipped away to the wash-tub, and the house smelt o' the hot iron the same as afore. The child was a puny, ailing little skiddick, and, what wi' wan thing and t'other, Job began to lose patience wi' life. He'd sit all day down to the Red Lion a-

sipping at his glass, only instead o' warming
his heart, the spirit kind o' tarned un sour.
Us niver got no free drinks from un, though
I, for one, missed the man's cheerful ways
more'n the ale: still, 'twadn't altogether sat-
isfactory to lose touch o' Mary Amelia's
earnings jest when winter was beginning to
shape. Zometimes the lads wud try and
draw Job on to talk o' women-folk; but he
zim'd to ha' lost faith, and zee'd 'em eye to
eye much the same as the rest o' us. I
thought to mezulf that 'twas curious the way
things falled out, for I had growed to respact
Mary Amelia out o' ordinary.

Wan night, jest as I was drapping off to
zlape, I was brought back to attention by
the sound o' a sharp cry. I zot up in bed
and listened, but naught came o' it, zo I
closed my eyes and didn't unbutton 'em
again till morning. Mary Amelia was standing aside her door when I went to my work
at daybreak: her whisked round and was
out o' sight in a minute, but not afore I had

zee'd an ugly black bruise on the face o' her.
"Job iddn't the sort that 'ud raise his hand
against a woman," I said to myzulf.   Down
to Dore Apple the men beat their wives regular, and 'twadn't long afore I learned
that Job had taken to do the zame.   Maybe
that zich conduct didn't no·ways surprise
Mary Amelia, for arter that first night her
niver called out, though many a time I've
zot up in bed and listened, sort o' anxious,
for, baing single, I'd had no taste o' the ag-
gravation o' women.   Dunstable Weir con-
sidered itzulf a cut above Dore Apple, and
no wan in our village had been known to do
more'n threaten his wife wi' the stick; so
when bit by bit the neighbours began to sus-
pect how things was atween Job and Mary
Amelia, they felt sore wi' 'em both.   There's
no doubt that Job wud ha' been axed to
leave straight away had folks been sure
there was truth in the tale.   They questioned
me time and again, but I niver told 'em
aught: if Mary Amelia held to silence, there

zim'd no reason for me to complain. Somehow, I think she suspicioned that I was her friend, though her always tarned a proud face on me, the same as her did to the rest. How hard the poor woman worked in they days! Many's the time I've thought to myzulf, "Mary Amelia desarves a peaceful old age more'n most."

Well, a matter o' dree years hiked by, and naught happened worth the mention, and then, wan winter's night as I zot rubbing a bit o' grease on my boots, there was a pull at the latch, and who should walk in but Mary Amelia. Things had been gwaying from bad to worse over opposite. I hadn't been nigh the cottage for a week or more, for I felt that an extry pair o' eyes be throwed away when a man has no business to mind but his own, and I knowed that Mary Amelia was much o' my mind, though her never put tongue to wuds to say so. Howsomever, there her stood, looking terrible piteous out o' her as-usual eye.

"Zack," her said, "the child's sick."

"Poor little skiddick! Shall I go for the doctor?"

"No, 'tiddn't that," her answered, stopping quat.

The clock in the corner struck ten, and as the hands stretched theirzulves past the hour I saw her glance round tremorful towards the street.

"'Tis closing time down to the Red Lion," her said.

I knowed then her wor afraid o' Job's distarbacious ways.

"The child's now but falled azleep," her continued. "I wouldn't have her woke sudden for worlds, and the men-folk make a deal o' clatter trapezing past the house."

Tremmy's was the last cottage on our side o' the village, so there wadn't no wan but Job likely to come this way. I didn't make no comment, but vallered her acrass to her cottage, though how I was to keep Job out o' his own home was more'n I could fathom.

Howsomever, when us got inside, there he was, and the sight o' un took Mary Amelia back considerable. It didn't need a second glance at Job's face to zee that, though not sober, he wadn't no more than what you might call friendly drunk; and pleased enough I was to mark that the sour look had gone from his eyes, for I thought to mezulf that wi' management things would settle down comfortable for the night. I hadn't reckoned wi' the accumulation o' merriment that was in the man, for what wi' having been on the cross so long, and what wi' being by nature vivacious, naught would satisfy Job but that Mary Amelia should stand up then and there and start dancing. Now, there was little o' the light fantastic about Mary Amelia, and when her had taken off her boots, and fixed her eye on the zlap-ing child, her heaved that poor ungainly body o' hers up and down; Job, he fell to laughing fair to split his sides, though, may-be becase he wadn't so drunk as us gave un

credit for, he did most o' his merriment zilent. Plazed to see that the child zlept on
undistarbed, Mary Amelia capered wonderful to behold. The moon riz and shone
down 'pon tap us all. All-to-wance the
child gave a bit o' a sigh, opened its eyes, and
looked from wan to t'other o' us sort o'
wearied. I thought for certain 'twud start
and bawl, but no; tired, maybe, o' the antics
o' this world, the little skiddick drapped
back wance more on the pilly, buttoned up
its little eyes, and jest died right there in
front o' us all.

'Twas done so unostentatious-like that
Mary Amelia didn't fathom first o' long
what the child had been arter. When her
did, she drapped down aside the cradle wonderful unnoiseful and laid her plainzome
face agin the plainzome face o' her child. I
went back home, for I cudn't do no good by
biding.

'Twadn't long arter that that Job Tremmy
falled out o' the back o' a cart and broke his

neck. A good riddance, most folk thought,
though I cudn't help baing a bit zarry, having known the man these many years and
more. Mary Amelia took widowhood as
her took most things, zilent. Not that her
neglected her husband now he was dead, for
her borrowed Varmer Burden's pony and
trap, drove over to Bideford and bought a
wonderful shiny tombstone into Mr. Baker's, wi'

> " Sorely tried, and gone before,
>   You've falled on earth, you fall no more,"

written on it in gold lettering picked out
wi' red. Everywan in the village held that
this was doing the thing handsome.

After the vust Zunday her went back to
work, and washed and starched away harder
than ever. Zometimes I'd drap in and
watch her o' an evening, and the thought
wud come over me that I'd like to zee they
worn red hands o' hers idle for a while. I'd
niver been no marrying man mezulf, the

maid I fancied not fancying me; but, bit by
bit, as the weeks went on, the idee kind o'
growed in my heart to up and marry Mary
Amelia. Howsomever, I wadn't gwaying to
do nothing rash, and when I walked up to
Varmer Burden wan Zunday to talk the
matter over wi' he, us counted no less than
saxteen widdies in the parish o' Dunstable
Weir, letting alone Dore Apple, that wud
ha' been only too willing to hang up their
bonnets in my back kitchen. Be that as it
may, I didn't tummil to none o' 'em: they
was a fast lot, most, and having worried
their Joes into the grave, wud ha' liked to
do the zame by me. Mary Amelia was a
different sort altogether, and I had a mind
to give her the taste o' a quiet life. " Her
shall larn what 'tis to have a man that don't
drink to fend for," I said to mezulf, and
wi' they wuds on my lips I hiked right
acrass to Tremmy's cottage and axed her to
be my wife.

The widdy listened to all I had to zay

wonderful unconsarned, which, taking into
consideration that her was more than usual
plainzome for a woman, made me veel jest a
small bit sore. Howsomever, I'm willun to
admit I shudn't ha' troubled much over the
matter if her hadn't flung my own looks in
my face.

"Zack," her said, "you'll make no personable second arter my poor Job."

Well, thought I, and that from a woman
vaytured the like o' her ! I didn't make no
comment, holding that a man can't court and
be testy at wan and the zame time; but it
sort o' comed over me that, whativer good
qualities Mary Amelia had, gratitude wadn't
wan o' 'em. Then I kained acrass at they
wored-out hands o' hers, and the sight o' 'em
called to my mind what scant cause the poor
soul had iver had to be grateful. Well, arter
a deal o' pressing, Mary Amelia consented to
marry me. The neighbours were a bit sniffy
over it, reckoning that I wanted to sit idle
while her worked herzulf to death: and

though I told 'em her wadn't gwaying to put a hand to any outside job when wance wife o' mine, they none o'em believed a wud o' what I said. I had been in regular work since a long time back, and, not baing a spending man, had managed to lay by a tidy bit. The week us was gwaying to be married I took the money out from a hole in the wall where I'd laid it, and bought some new fixings for the kitchen, also a Bible and a feather fan to stand on the table in the parlour windy; but afore I fetched a stick o' the furniture home from Bideford I set to and white-washed the cottage inside and out. I axed Varmer Burden to drap in when 'twas all fixed up tidy, which he did.

"Well, Zack," says he, casting a sort o' unzeeing eye round, "I niver thought to zee 'ee mated; but there, the women be all for marrying, no matter who 'tis.

I showed un the Bible and the feather fan; he zim'd too much taken up in thought to note 'em.

The neighbours all comed to the wedding, and us had a wonderful lot o' gifts, mostly chiney dogs for the mantelshelf, though wan man from Dore Apple who had been in furren parts made Mary Amelia a present o' a small poisonous eel in a glass box half full o' mud. Sich a gift had never been zeen in the village afore, and folks agreed that there must be a meaning to it, and 'twud be certain sure to bring us good luck; so me and Mary Amelia us each took hold o' the little glass box wi' a finger and thumb, and carried un in and laid un on the parlour table atween the Bible and the feather fan.

Us was married on a Saturday, and the vallering Monday morning I got up and dressed myzulf as zoon as iver it was light, went down to the back yard, took up my axe, and then and there I split Mary Amelia's wash-tubs into small pieces only fit for firing. I was jest making the chips up into bundles when who should come into the yard but Mary Amelia.

"Law, Zack!" her said, "wheriver did 'ee get all they nice dry chips?"

"Out o' your old wash-tubs," I answered, kind o' unconsarned, for, arter all, when I comed to think o' it, 'twas a spendthrift thing to do.

Mary Amelia didn't fathom what I meant. "I never saw no chips there overnight," her said.

"They was wash-tubs then."

"Be 'ee daft, Zack?"

"No, Mary Amelia," I answered, "I bain't daft; but I want to zee they hands o' yours idle for a bit, that's all."

Her stood kaining terrible lonezome-like down on the bits o' chips.

"I've been used to work all my life," her said, and went into the house wi'out another wud. When I came back from work at dinner-time her eyes were red and swollen, jest for all the world as if her had been crying past belief.

"Well," thought I to myzulf, "'tiddn't al·ways kindness that fetches."

Mary Amelia wadn't wan o' they that get fat on idleness, for each month that hiked by left her thinner and more sorry-looking than the last, till there was times when I wondered to myzulf if her got up and worked while I was azlape. Wan night I bided awake jest to zee what her might be arter; but, beyond sighing, her didn't do naught. I woke her up and axed what her was sighing the like o' that for. Her falled all o' a tremble. That's what comes o' marrying a woman used to the feel o' the stick!

"I iddn't gwaying to touch 'ee, Mary Amelia," I said, proud to be minded that I was a different sort o' man altogether from Job.

A kind o' resigned look staled acrass the vace o' her, and I thought to myzulf, "Poor soul, her's still mixating me up 'long o' the dead." But her wadn't.

"Let me zlape, Zack," her said; "for then if I fret, leastways I don't knaw o' it."

"What have 'ee got to fret over, Mary Amelia?" I axed. "Haven't I bided by my wud and tooked good care o' 'ee?"

"Ay, the best o' care," her answered.

"Well, zlape and forgit you war iver married to t'other man."

She closed her eyes weariful. "Ess, I'm always glad o' a bit o' zlape," her said, and wi' that her buttoned up her eyes wance again.

The vallering day when I comes back from work I marked a smell o' spirits about. When I axed Mary Amelia if her noted aught, she said that her'd been mending an old suit o' Job's clothes. I didn't make no comment, becase Job had drunk so 'mazing much in his time, it might well be that his clothes still leaked o' the liquor. Howsomever, the weeks went on, and I was a bit surprised to find the smell o' spirits as markful as iver, and I told Mary Amelia to hang the clothes on the line or else give over mending 'em. But her answered that fresh air didn't

make no impression on Job's coats and weskits, though the cloth was too good to be
drowed away. Being a careful man, I didn't
say no more, and the matter passed from my
mind, till wan day old Varmer Burden
stapped me in Mucksey Lane, where I had a
bit o' a job, hedging and ditching.

"Zack," says he, laying wan o' they banging great hands o' his 'pon tap my shoulder,
"what be this tale I hears o' 'ee having
taken to drink on the quiet?"

"I don't know naught o' sich tales," I answered. "I've niver been nigh the Red
Lion since the day I was married."

"Maybe," he said; "but you sends your
wife there to get drink for 'ee reg'lar. I've
seen her come out o' the public more'n wance
myzulf." I was that took aback I couldn't
find wuds, and Varmer Burden let slide the
hand from off my shoulder. "'Twud ha'
been a better-sized consarn if you'd fetched
the drink yourzulf," he said.

"I'll thank 'ee to mind your own business," I answered, tarning back wance more to work; but he wadn't no-ways satisfied.

"Who cud her git the drink for if 'twadn't for 'ee, Zack?" he said, sort o' 'pologising.

I laughed sharp out. "I shall drink when and how I've a mind to," and wi' that Varmer Burden was fo'ced to be content, for not a wud more cud he git out o' me. When he was gone I let fall the billhook out o' my hand, swarmed up an old allum that grew 'pon tap the bank, and kained acrass to where my cottage stud, the best part o' a mile away. The smoke was creeping up droo the trees, and the little bit o' a place looked powerzome unconsarned. I cud most zee Mary Amelia in the big chair azide the dresser, where her had tooked to sitting o' late. There was a deal o' waiting to be passed over afore the church clock struck sax and I was free to put up my tools and go back along home. I tarned over to myzulf what I shud zay, but I hadn't got no forrader wi' the wuds when the big bell

telled out the hour. I put my things togither and started, fast fust o' all, then zlow-
ing down. It comed over me that 'twud be
as well to go in by the front door and kind
o' take Mary Amelia unaware. Howsomever, I went in at the back the zame as usual,
only maybe I was a bit longer putting away
my tools, becase they falled all o' a heap on
the stone pavement and made sich a clatter
that Mary Amelia comed to the windy to zee
what the noise was about. There wadn't no
tea ready, but I was willun to wait, not baing over and above hungry. Wan o' Job's
weskits lay 'pon tap the table, smelling terrible barefaced o' spirits. I had a mind to
drow the weskit into the fire and be done wi'
the stench wance and for all, but zommat
made me hold my hand. Arter all, there
wadn't much to be said agin a bit o' a weskit. Mary Amelia went out to fill the kettle
at the pump, and I thought maybe 'twud be
as well to give a look inside the dresser.
Howsomever, I wadn't sharp enough, for her

comed back in afore I'd stirred a stap from
where I stud. When us had had tea and
the things had been cleared away, I took my
week's wages and laid the whole o' it in
Mary Amelia's hand. Her looked down at
the money sort o' mixed, curious and eager,
becase, afore this, I'd niver gived her more'n
a part o' what I had arned.

" You didn't reckon on it being so much ? "
I axed.

" No," her answered. " You arn a higher
wage than I thought."

" Mary Amelia," I said, sort o' earnest,
" since me and you have got married, I've
strove as I've never strove afore. I want
to zee 'ee comfortable and cared for.
You've had a deal to put up with in your
time, but I don't ax more o' 'ee than to do
the best you can by yourzulf."

Her tarned the money over and over afore
answering, then her drowed it down on the
table. " Why do 'ee give me such a deal all-
to-wance ? " her said, resentful-like.

" 'Tis safer wi' 'ee than lying about in my pocket."

Us was both zilent for a long while arter that, then Mary Amelia comed acrass to where I zot.

" Let me go back to wark, Zack," her said. " I was niver made for an idle woman."

'Twadn't comfortzome to hear her talk zo, for I'd set my heart on her having an easy time ; but life is a quare consarn, and 'tiddn't always the softest cushion that makes the softest seat.

" Do as it plazes 'ee best, Mary Amelia," I said.

Her put wan o' her wored-out hands 'pon tap o' mine. " 'Tis more'n money 'ee be giving me, now, Zack," her answered, and wi' that us both went upstairs to bed.

Well, the wash-tubs wance bought, the ginelfolks was only too willun to send in their fallals. As for Mary Amelia, her packed away Job's weskits in the old press in the attic, and the cottage took agin to smelling o' the hot iron.

Varmer Burden was that plazed wi' the way things had falled out, that he stapped me wan Zunday arternoon ez I was gwaying into charch and shook me by the hand.

"I always zed, Let the right man take 'ee the right way, you wud pull up, Zack," he tumm'l'd out, and, not waiting for an answer from me, he stalked into charch, content, no doubt, to take his praise from the hands o' the Almighty Hiszulf.

It takes zommat more'n the past to make the present, howzomiver, and 'twadn't long afore I larned that Mary Amelia's washing didn't give the satisfaction that it had done wance. Her hadn't the zame use o' her iron, and her feel for starch wadn't so sure as it had been in the old days. The ginelfolks were slow to leave her; but, bit by bit, their custom went elsewhere, till at last naught but stray furreners' trash comed our ways at all. It zim'd cruel like that a few

years' idleness shud wark sich a change in a
woman's power, and I knaw'd well enough
that in her heart o' hearts Mary Amelia laid
the blame at my door. Her didn't zay
naught—'twadn't her nater to cast hard
thoughts at a man, but her kind o' felt the
more, sucking a deal o' furren feeling out
o' the zilence. I always larned when the
ginelfolks had been angered wi' her, becase
it was her custom at sich times to take
Job's spiritous-smelling weskit out o' the
press and lay it sort o' bare-faced on the
kitchen table. 'Twadn't often folks dropped
in our way : now and again Varmer Burden
would tie his nag to the fence and let fall a
few wuds. He comed wance when Mary
Amelia was by herzulf, and took the trouble
to ride all round by Mucksey Lane to tell
me that the house was a long way off baing clean. I said, what wi' the washing and
wan thing and t'other, Mary Amelia hadn't
time to mind sich things ; but he answered
'twas well known in the village that Mary

Amelia's washing wadn't a patch on what it had been in Job's time, and no wan sent her work on thic account.

I didn't zay no more, though 'tiddn't over and above pleasant to hear sich wuds from a neighbour's lips. Arter thic day I niver laid the whole o' my arnings in Mary Amelia's hand, but kept part o' the wage to ha' zommat to vall back on. There was a bit o' white-wash over from the last time I did down the walls; so I got up early the next morning and put a fresh coat on 'em, and gave a stroke or two o' green paint to the windies. A pedler chanced to pass by jest as I was giving the finishing touch, so I called un acrass and bought a row of chiney jugs—for Mary Amelia had a loose-vingered hand wi' sich o' late. Her comed in herzulf and stud watching, none too plazed I cud tell by the way her had o' wiping her dry hands on her apron—a trick o' hers when put out.

"Whativer be 'ee making all this to-do for, Zack?" her axed.

" I'm getting things a bit vitty for 'ee."

" Wadn't they to your taste afore? "

" A good wife desarves a good home."

But Mary Amelia wadn't no friend to
mealy-mouthed folk.

" I've niver been a good wife to 'ee," her
rapped out sharp, "and, what's more, flum-
mery won't make me wan."

Then her tarned on her heel and went upstairs. I was fo'ced to git my own breakfast and hike to wark wi' naught in the
basket to stand atween me and sax o'clock.
It fell out that I met Varmer Burden ez I
was coming home along from wark, and,
knowing that the house was looking out o'
usual vitty, I axed un, sort o' casual, to drop
in and git some bulbs he fancied. Us
hadn't got more'n than lifted the latch o' the
gate when, what shud I zee bang in the
middle o' the path, like a sign-post wi' BE-
WARE writ on it, but Job's weskit. I
stapped quat, and wud ha' axed Varmer Burden to do the like, but he was plump inside

the cottage afore I had time to open my mouth.

'Twadn't more than wan step acrass the threshold he took afore he whipped round and waited for me to join un, which I was amazing slow to do.

"There's been a royal smash-up here," he said, sort o' beckoning me forward.

Sure anuff, the whole row of chiney jugs for which I'd paid four and ninepence thic morning lay in small pink bits 'pon tap the floor.

"'Tis that varmint o' a cat," I tummiled out, though, truth to tell, there wadn't no such thing about the place.

"I niver heard tell that you had a cat," said Varmer Burden.

"Begore, and I cud wish the zame! I was vule anuff to buy wan into Bideford," I answered, terrible smart—but there, a lie is always a fluid thing.

The door atween the kitchen and front room was a bit ajar, and at this identical

moment what shud I catch sight o' but Mary
Amelia herzulf lying her length on the
parlour floor. I was that took back I cudn't
stir hand nor foot, and as I stud waiting for
the worst, there comed a banging great snore
bassooning droo the house.

"Whativer's that?" said the varmer,
drawing back a step.

"An old white owl in the parlour chimney," I answered.

"I niver heard tell that you had an owl in
your parlour chimney," said he, sort o' sus-
picious-like.

"Law, ess," said I, "and a powerful
worrit her be."

Varmer Burden leaned forward till I
thought for sure he must vall on that long,
pointed, curious nose o' his.

"Whativer's that?" he axed, pointing his
vinger at wan o' Mary Amelia's feet that
stretched past the crack o' the door.

"A boot," I said.

"Be there a fut in it?"

"Have'n 'ee iver seen a boot by itzulf afore?"

"Not up-ended the zame as thic."

All-to-wance the boot twitched back out o' sight.

"There be a fut in it," said Varmer Burden, sort o' triumphal.

"And the meazles as well," I put in.

"What!" said the old varmer, jumping a good dree feet backwards droo the doorway. "Whyiver didn't 'ee tell me that afore?"

"Becase I've always heard tell that you was scart out o' your life o' the disease."

He didn't wait to hear further, and when I made sarten that I had zee'd the last o' un, I went out the house and locked the door behind me.

A matter o' twelve miles up the river was the parish o' Little Dunstable. 'Twas there that I was born, and as I locked the door ahind me, the thought comed droo my head that I wud dearly like to zee the little place wance again. I stapped acrass to ax my

master for a day's leave, and he said I might
make it two. The moon stud in her third
quarter, and as I was minded to walk to Little Dunstable that night, I didn't waste no
time in starting. I had a brother, a cobbler,
who lived about a mile on this side o' the
village, and I thought maybe that, being
wan o' the family, I might spake out a bit
fuller to he than to t'other folks. Howzomiver, though I stayed into the second day, I
didn't say naught to un, and I wadn't altogether zarry to tarn my vace home along
once more. My heart gi'ed a bit o' a blob
when I catched sight o' my cottage agin,
and I cudn't but wonder what Mary Amelia
wud ha' to say. No smoke peered sort o'
expecting droo the trees, but I'd growed
used to finding the fire out. The little
gate was off the hinges and lay on its back
azide the road, as forlorn as a capsized duck.
Bits o' straw and paper littered the garden,
and the flowers was trampled past uprising.
I stud gapnesting round, the like o' any fur-

ren loon, then I took dree banging great steps and thrust open the door o' the cottage.

"Mary Amelia!" I hammered out.

But there wadn't no Mary Amelia. Naught but the bare walls and boards. Her had gone, and took every stick o' the furniture 'long wi' her.

I niver vallered her up to try and git the things back, though I knawed that, according to the law, a married woman hadn't got no claim to more'n her gold ring and the bit o' bootlace her ties her hair wi'; but Varmer Burden told me he had catched sight o' her wance into Barnstaple, and he added zommat that has made bad blood atween he and me.

Dree years ago last Christmas her comed back. 'Twas a wild-featured night, raining and blowing anuff to scare most folks into keeping atween the blankets. I was zlaping 'pon tap a couple o' boards I'd nailed to a spare box or two. Baing by nature a careful man, I'd niver made no outlay on furni-

ture zince Mary Amelia wadn't in need o'
aught from me. When fust I heard the
knock on the door I was for biding where I
was, but there was zommat in the feeble,
clapperting zound that kind o' minded me
o' the lonezomeness o' the world outzide. I
pulled on an extry pair o' trousers, for the
cold wadn't to be denied, slipped acrass the
kitchen, and opened the door. A blast o'
wind swirled round the bare room and out
agin, taking the light wi' it, and I was fo'ced
to go to the mantelshelf to fumble for a
fresh match. My fingers was all thumbs,
and I cudn't make naught out o' the lucifers;
yet, though 'twas too dark to zee aught, I
kind o' suspicioned who it was that had
come in on me thic sudden.

"Mary Amelia, do 'ee reckon you cud git
a light out o' the blamed sticks?" I axed,
sharp-like.

She took the box from my hand and
struck a match, and us looked wan into
t'other's vace. A shiver ran droo me,

though maybe 'twas zommat more'n cold that gripped hold o' my heart jest then.

" I haven't got no right to come back to 'ee, Zack," her said.

My lips got sort o' trembly, and the wuds fell back unspoke.

" 'Tis a wild night for 'ee to be out in, Mary Amelia," I answered, arter a bit.

Her leaned agin the dresser and coughed zommat fearzome to hearken to. All-to-wance she zim'd to slip and vall sideways on the floor. When I bent over to raise her up, I zee'd a little stream o' blood thread itzulf acrass her lips; I lifted her on to the bed and was for fetching the doctor, but her wadn't have me go.

" Tiddn't no manner o' use, Zack," her said. " I shud be dead afore he comed, and there's thic that I must tell 'ee."

Wi' that, her fell zilent for a terrible number o' minutes. I kept piling on all my spare clothes 'pon tap of her poor, trembly body, for, though I wud ha' gi'ed a

deal to help her jest then, I never was wan
to know the right thing to do when took by
surprise.

A bit o' a smile comed into her vace;
maybe her suspicioned I was wishful o' plaz-
ing her.

"You was always willun, Zack," her
said.

"I be zlow to larn, Mary Amelia," I answered, taking her hand. She gripped it
close; then her head falled back, and I
thought that all was over wi' her, poor soul.
But wance more her opened her eyes.

I stooped down and placed my ear close
to her lips.

"You should ha' taken the stick to me,
Zack," her murmured. "When iverything
went agin me, I was rispacted *then*."

"I rispact 'ee, Mary Amelia," I said.
"I've always rispacted 'ee."

"'Twudn't be right to rispact me now,"
her answered; "for I be—"

Death took the wuds from her lips, and

though I cried out arter her terrible loud, I doubt if she heard.

No matter, the Almighty knaws that there be folks that rispact Mary Amelia Spot.

THE SISTERS

JUST where the river took her last turn to the right afore swishing past the village o' Dunstable Weir, two small cottages stood up pink and straight wi' a row o' allums on the sky-line ahind 'em. They were built stone for stone the same, were called The Sisters, and two sisters lived in 'em whose married name was Barnaby, though their husbands wadn't no-ways related. Martha Barnaby, the elder, was a widdy by will, her man bein' friendly to furren parts. She was a thin, scant-featured woman, wi' a head unsuspicious o' hair, which didn't prevent her from having a fine notion o' how to pickle bacon. There were no children in her house, though a little extry room had been walled up special for sich; but into Susan's was a snip o' a lad called

Jerry for short, he being held over the font to the name o' Jerulam. The wall that parted the two cottages wadn't over thick, most could be heard through it, and folks say that it was the sound o' Jerry's first puling cry that hardened Martha's heart agin her sister. Be that as it may, her was a changed woman from that time on, and wud tarn from a child's face much as if it was thic o' the Evil Wan hiszulf. The lad's mother didn't take no count o' the matter, reckoning things wud mend wi' time, though mor'n wan pussen counselled her to keep an eye on Jerry lest evil should befall un; but Susan laughed in the face o' 'em all, reckoning that she knowed her sister better than to waste time over such add-two-to-wan work. Arter thic the village held silent, part becase if words fell loose about Susan her husband was niver hit by 'em, John Barnaby laying away from most things, his mind being sort o' tarned in upon itzulf; and part that the village couldn't help but be a bit curious to see what might befall if things was left to take their own course. Well, the years went on till Jerry had seen eight springs and seven falls o' the year—and Martha becoming more and more queer in the temper all the while. 'Twas his birthday and a fine blustercacious morning in March wi' the sap rising in the trees fair to bust the bark off 'em, and Susan, her gi'ed the basket wi' her husband's dinner into Jerry's hand, and told the lad to take it acrass to where John Barnaby was felling trees a good mile up on the hither side o' the river. Her niver set eyes on the lad agin 'til the water washed un round the bend and into the shaller where her stood, ankle-deep, rinsing a roll o' linen afore laying it out in the sun to bleach. Her took the child up in her arm and carried un to the cottage. When her comed nigh the door, who should rush past her, dripping from head to heel, but Martha. For a banging great minute the two sisters stud and looked each into

t'other's eyes, then Martha let fly wan o' her
mad-house laughs, and bust away back acrass
the meadow, cackling as her went. There
wadn't a pussen inside the village or out,
saving, maybe, mezulf, but held that Martha
had drowned the child. The perlice didn't
move, sich folk being paid reg'lar, wark or
no wark, but 'twadn't for want o' hearing o'
wan suspicioned o' the crime. An inquest
was held down at the Red Lion, folks spoke
a deal that the crowner said wadn't evidence,
and the jury brought it in that the child was
dead sure as a gun, but further than thic
they wadn't in the position to clarify. That
night, howsomever, the village painted "Mur-
deress" in red paint acrass the staps o' Martha's door. John Barnaby runned up to my
house to ax for a drap o' turpentine to take
out the stain afore the dumman catched
sight o' the wuds. He didn't say naught to
me then, and I niver was wan for axing
questions, holding that 'tis the silent man
that hears most; but when I tarned into the

Red Lion thic evening for a glass o' ale, the zame as is usual wi' me, he comed to the bar windy and sort o' beckoned, till I rose and hiked out to un.

"Zack," he says, "I can't talk to 'ee here. Let us go into the fields."

I vallered un acrass a wonderful lot o' land till us got bang in the middle o' wan o' the squire's woods, then he whipped round all o' a sudden.

"I shall be fo'ced to tull," he tumm'led out.

"The poor soul knaws well anuff her hadn't no hand in drowning the chile," I answered.

"Susan don't knaw. I shall be fo'ced to tull her."

I hadn't wuds to answer he, but I eyed un sort o' hasty, and, though the night was dark past zeeing aught, I kind o' suspicioned the look that was on the vace o' un. It started to rain, sofy vust along, than more willun. The draps comed slattering down

as us stood there zilent, and it zim'd to me
that he was axing agin and agin the zame
question.

"Must I tell her?" he zim'd to ask.

But no zound comed from his lips, and I
made as though I hadn't heard.

Then zommat goaded un on agin. He scut
away droo the trees and comed out on a big
barley mow; wance there, he tarned his vace
down stream and runned toward his own
cottage like a pussen possessed, and I arter
un for want o' aught better to do. The
Sisters stood terrible snug under their
thatch, wi' jest anuff glint from the moon to
show where wan cottage ended and t'other
began. John Barnaby pulled up thic short
that I was 'pon tap un afore I could stop
mezulf.

"Zack," he says, "go and look into the
windy. Tippy-toe."

"Whose windy? Susan's?" I axed.

He nodded his head, and I stole forrard
sort o' crippled and stared in 'pon tap the
poor dumman.

"What shall I do now I be here?" I axed in a whisperation voice.

"Be her busy over zommat or jest making believe to work?"

"Her's moving round considerable, but wat her be arter I can't rightly surmise."

At that he fell zilent a bit. "Her's trying to put a different vace on things," he zed at last.

"'Twull take more than the movething o' chairs and tables to do thic," I thought to mezulf as I stood gapnesting droo the windy. The rain was falling thick, and I could zee the lights o' the Red Lion acrass the water. It zim'd a drearzome, lack-sense business standing there in the wet, so I creep'd back to John.

"I reckon," I zed, "I'll be gitting home along."

His vingers closed on my arm. "If 'twas no but the village I had to tell, not her," he whispered.

"Her'll be less hard on 'ee than the village," I answered.

" The village iddn't no mother, the village haven't lost no chile," he said, coming forrard to the windy and drawing me 'long wi' un.

Her had got herzulf down and was staring out droo the lattice, though twad at zommat other than us, no doubt.

John shivered. " 'Tiddn't no use standing here," he zed. " If I must tell her, I must."

" Ess, go in and git it over," I answered, plazed to be quit o' the job—but he tarned on me sort o' fierce.

" You'll come in along o' me. Maybe you can throw in an easying wud."

" 'Twud be a poor show if dree pussens played in it," I zed, edging away from un.

But he wudn't be persuaded. " Step inside for a bit," he answered. " As like as not I sha'n't zay aught while 'ee be there."

Zo I vallered un in.

Susan riz her head and kind o' smiled at un.

" Have 'ee been lonezome ? " he axed.

" Not over and above," her answered.

" But 'ee have been missing the child ? "

Her kind o' tarned from the question. " The house be most too quiet when you be away to work, John," her zed.

He comed across to where her zot. " Susan," he tumm'led out all-to-wance, " 'twad all along o' me that Jerry was drowned thic day."

Her riz up wonderful slow, and then zot down, heap-like, but nary a wud crassed her lips.

John Barnaby tarned his vace from her, and went on wi' his tale quick, as if he feared that wance stapped short in it he wud bide zilent to the crack o' doom.

" 'Twad jest above the willows he fell in; where folks zay the water don't come much over a man's waist. The stream slewed un round, and he held out his arms to me and gav' a little scrit o' a cry. I ran to the side and was minded to jump in, but zommat held me there watching, though I knowed if I wadn't smart the river 'ud snatch un away. 'Twadn't more'n a minute that I bided kind o' humped togither, ready to jump, then the river snatched un, and he slithied into midstream. For a bit his little white face lay 'pon tap the water, and I runned along the bank, bawling out that I wud save un yit; but I niver got nigh un, I was afear'd o' the water."

He stopped quat and the room was painful zilent.

I wud ha' up and hiked, but there was thic about the zilence that bound me back from the breaking o' it. No wan minded on me, they had zommat other to think on. John, he comed forward to where his wife zot.

"I cud ha' saved un, but I was afear'd," he said. "I wadn't smart enough. God Almighty gi'ed me jest wan minute. I heard His voice plain as I be speaking to 'ee. 'John,' He zed, 'don't waste time. Jump,' He zed. I was minded to jump later. I niver was well plucked on the instant."

He stapped short and held out his hands towards her, sort o' trembly.

"You'll always remember that I cud ha' saved un, Susan?" he asked, wistful like.

But her didn't answer he a wud.

"'Tis sort o' natural that 'ee shud mind on thic," he harped on.

Then her spoke. "Wat wull 'ee do now?"

He wiped the sweat off his vace. "I've told 'ee, Susan, there be no but the village to tull, and they bain't much count."

Her zot up smart. "The village," her zed. "Wull 'ee tull the village that 'ee as good as killed your own child?"

Wance again he put out his hands sort o' pleadful, but he didn't zay naught, and Susan drapped her vace down 'pon tap the table. "Jerry, my little lad, my Jerry, my child, my heart. Why didn't the Almighty call on me to save 'ee? My little lad, I wudn't ha' let the cold water take hold o' 'ee. You shud ha' gone warm to death agin my breast."

John tarned and walked sort o' tottery tow-ards the door, but he hadn't movetted far afore her was up and arter un.

"Where be 'ee gwaying?" her cried, sharp-like.

"To tull 'em."

"Be 'ee stark mad that you shud tull 'em sich?"

"Zack can tull 'em, he wor there—"

"Zack?"

"Ess, he saw the lad drown."

Her tarned to where I zot, and I riz up from my sate, for there was thic in her vace that wud ha' stirred the dead.

"You crawling toad on two legs!" her cried. "Do 'ee call yerzulf a man to stand and zee a chile drown afore 'ee eyes? The village shall know 'ee for the murderer you are. Don't 'ee reckon to escape, I'll denounce 'ee to the Law."

"Zack was t'other side o' the stream."

"And what difference does that make?" her answered, vacing round on her husband.

" He can't swim four strokes, the zame ez mezulf."

" Swim," her zed, "swim ! A murderer hadn't no need for swimming, he can murder wi'out thic," and zot herzulf down 'pon tap the nearest chair, flung her apron over her head, and fell to crying painful to witness. I tippy-toed out. It zim'd a murderous thing to ha' watched a chile drown and niver so much as to ha' jumped in arter it, swim or no swimy.

Wat wi' wan thing and t'other, I didn't zlape over well thic night, and glad enough I was when the dark had been rubbed out o' the sky and the world took to looking usual-like. I didn't waste no time over breakfast, becase I had a fancy to go as far as the Barnabys and have a glance in on 'em, my work lying a bit on their side o' the village. 'Twas a grey morning, the mist had stretched itzulf between the hills, and the valley looked most as if there was a river o' smoke instead o' water running droo her.

I kept along the track, and when I comed nigh the Barnabys' cottage, I heard voices, though I cudn't zee who was father to the clatter. Stapping short, kind o' instinctive, I catched hold o' the sound o' John's thick tongue, which was dabbling about in his throat much as if he had swallered more mist than honest breakfast. He wor speaking to Martha. I edged a bit closer, for I was marvellous curious to know what he and her had to tull wan to t'other.

"I niver let on to her that you jumped into the water arter un. I sort o' forgot," he zed.

There wadn't no answer, and I cud hear John Barnaby's vingers cracking like the bustling o' the ash buds on a still night. Arter a bit he spoke agin.

"I've been most 'mazin' long tulling her how 'twas."

"Have 'ee told her?" Martha axed, sharp-like.

"I was fo'ced."

" Fo'ced, was 'ee ? "

" Ess, becase her suspicioned that some-wan t'other than me had done it."

" And now 'ee be gwaying to tull the village ? "

" Ess."

" Be 'ee fo'ced to do thic too ? "

" I was niver afear'd o' what the village might think."

" They'll cast it at 'ee that you let your own chile drown afore your eyes."

" Ess," he answered, " I let un drown. I cudn't ha' believed it agin mezulf if anywan was to ha' told me so afore it happened."

" Nor I that I shud ha' tried to save un. Us be different from what us thinks, all o' us," her zed.

" He's dead now, anyway."

" Many's the time I wished un so."

" I loved un, though it zims 'twas a poor sort o' love."

Her movetted a bit closer to John. "'Twadn't longer ago than last year that I

was nigh on pushing Jerry into the river at
the very identical spot that the water took
un."

"And yit 'twas you, not me, that tried to
save the lad."

"I wudn't worrit over it, John Barnaby,"
her answered sort o' solemn. "God Almighty knows our hearts better than us do
ourzulves."

"God Almighty may forgit it, but Susan
niver will," he zed, zarrerful.

"Her had the bearing o' the lad."

"'Twas a proud day for her when first he
laid agin her heart. 'John,' her zed, 'us
will call un Jerulam, 'tis a name that the
village hasn't took.' So us called un thic,
though the passon wor agin the name on the
score that 'twas high-fangled."

"He was a small baby," Martha answered,
"and cried a deal for a single chile. Many's
the time I've thought to mezulf that he
wadn't over well handled."

"I reckon I must be gwaying now," John
zed.

" Where be 'ee agwaying ? "

" To the village."

" What do 'ee want wi' the village ? "

" To tull 'em the truth how it was."

" Be 'ee a vule or a woman, John Barnaby, that you don't know the vally o' zilence ? "

" I be a man that let his own chile drown, that's what I be, Martha Barnaby."

" And will 'ee tell 'em thic ? "

" Ess," he answered, and hiked right away.

I cud hear un trapezing along at a fine rate. As for the old dumman, her stud gapnesting arter un droo the grey mist.

" Us be all afear'd o' different things," her zed, soft-like, then her tarned and went up the staps into Susan's house, and I vallered behind, sort o' tippy-toe.

" Wat be 'ee adoing here, Martha Barnaby ? " axed her sister, harsh-like. " You that hated the lad sore. Be 'ee come to gape at the empty chair that held un, and the bed whereon he laid ? "

" No, 'tiddn't for thic I've come," t'other

dumman answered, "for 'tis ill work looking for a chile that is being held back from 'ee, born or unborn."

"You be no bearer o' childer."

"My heart has sought arter a chile as your heart seeks arter Jerry now."

"How can 'ee knaw my heart's zarrer?"

Martha crossed the kitchen and stood over agin her sister.

"They be his shoes," her zed. "The lad had small feet; I marked that from the fust."

"Your eyes niver rested on the lad. How come 'ee to knaw that his feet were small?" her sister answered, harsh as iver.

"I kind o' saw 'em, though I tried not to zee un."

"There was always evil in your heart agin the lad."

"My heart was empty and hate growed there."

"Now my heart is empty and I hate 'ee becase 'ce hated the lad."

"Do 'ee mind his eyes? They was gold as water that runs acrass the brown moor sods."

"Who be you to name the colour o' his eyes?"

"I kind o' marked 'em, though I tried not to mark 'em."

"The river brought un back to me, but his eyes was closed—"

"And the smile gone from 'em."

"You niver zee'd un smile, for he was afear'd o' 'ee."

"Yit I kind o' knowed o' the smile."

"I shall niver zee un smile now."

"'Tis hid behind they long lashes o' un."

"Who be you to tell me how he zlapes?"

"He zlapes sound, no mother cud rock un to zo sound a zlape."

"Wud that I could zlape azide un."

"'Twud be a sweet rasting-place. I cud wish mezulf no better."

"Who be you to lie bezide my Jerry?"

"I have hungered for a chile these years."

Arter thic they fell zilent, both o' 'em. A breeze comed down from the head o' the valley and rolled the mist up the hillsides. I tarned sort o' instinctive and looked at the village, and as I stud gapnesting, John stapped over the stile, a power o' folk vallering un acrass the meadow. He walked along, his head bent, much like a man who held himzulf to be alone. Up the staps o' his own door he hiked, the crowd on the heels o' un, and mezulf at the rear o' the litter.

Susan Barnaby riz up from her sate and stared at us most 'mazing astonished.

" Be 'ee off your chump, John Barnaby ? " her axed, " that 'ee shud come here wi' all the trash o' the village trapezing at your heels ? "

" He zed 'twor he that murdered the chile," wan o' the crowd tumm'l'd out, sort o' uneasy.

" Gwaying from door to door tulling folk," put in another o' 'em.

Susan Barnaby sank back on her chair. "He'd tell up any tale, zarrer has tarned his head," she said, feeble-like.

"Us knawed all along 'twadn't more'n his fancy," the crowd answered.

"Zarrer has turned other heads azide his," Martha zed, half to herzulf.

But the crowd tarned on her, hungry-like. "You'd best bide quiet, Widdy Barnaby, or the rope 'ull 'ave 'ee yit."

"It has had many that desarved it less," her answered.

THE END.